A CHILD OF CARISTOKE:

BOOK TWO

THE SWORDS OF

AVAT'AR

L.F. CHIESA

A Child of Caristoke: Book 2. The Swords of Avat'ar. Copyright © 2026 by Flora Church.

Paperback edition: May 2026

ISBN 979-8-9997434-4-2 (paperback)

ISBN 979-8-9997434-5-9 (e-book)

www.emmacharles.net

For the first five, love you all

And for Teressa—larger than life itself

CHAPTER ONE

Caristoke

Clutching the basket of eggs carefully before him, Nickolas called good-bye to red-cheeked Dubby McFadol, his best friend. Seven years' old now, but as thin and blond and pale as ever, Nickolas' quick brown eyes scanned the street before him as he trotted on his way. Old enough to run errands for his mother alone, all his attention was concentrated on getting his cargo home safely. Too much so perhaps, for too late did he notice the skulking forms of Madowr Creavy and his moon-faced pal Wheedle Dermot sallying forth from the alley as he passed them.

"Yah! Yah! Nickolas!" Madowr taunted as his rough hands took the younger boy by the shoulders and twirled him about. Ferociously hanging onto his basket, Nickolas tried to squirm away. He might have made it if Wheedle, like a pointy-nosed rat, had not sidled up behind his bully of a friend and thrust a stick at Nickolas' flying feet.

Down he went hard on his knees, falling forward, the basket and its nested eggs crushed hopelessly before him. A lone surviving egg wobbled weakly across the cobbles. Dimly behind him he heard howls of laughter from Madowr and the snuffling swallowed laughter of Wheedle. Biting his lip to hold back the angry tears that smarted in his eyes, Nickolas came up from the ground with his chin jutting out and his balled fists raised before him.

A most astonishing sight met his eyes. Madowr's feet dangled in front of him as Wheedle, his stick forgotten, cowered in the street on quaking knees. Too frightened to run, he squeaked instead like the rodent he resembled.

"Speak, oh valiant young squire!" A deep voice he remembered well resounded high above his head. "What would you have me do with this most vile and errant knave?"

Sir Persiflas glared with disdain at the wretched form of Madowr that he held as he sat the sleek black warhorse Rex, and then shook his captive for good measure.

In spite of the carnage on the street behind him, Nickolas' mouth twitched and he smothered a giggle, so silly did Madowr and Wheedle look.

"I think, Sir Persiflas, you'd better let him go," he suggested, his words tinged with regret.

"A most judicious and fair-minded youth," Sir Persiflas declaimed in a loud voice, exhaling a great sigh. "With all his eggs broken and his knees scraped, he would let you go, though you are a most offensive miscreant!" Again the great mailed fist shook Madowr, whose eyes rolled from side to side as his arms and legs flailed the air.

"Forsooth, young Nickolas speaks well, oh Sir Knight!" Another voice answered, as familiar as the knight's. Nickolas' eyes widened and his grin near split his cheeks as a second rider appeared from behind the towering black charger.

"Hallo, Nickolas!" The merry blue eyes of Squire Daven twinkled as he winked at his young friend and brought Hesperius, his balky gray mule with its one brown eye and one blue eye to a halt.

"Hallo, Squire Daven!" Nickolas returned.

"Well, Sir Knight?" Squire Daven inquired of his comrade.

The knight heaved a great, mocking sigh.

"Very well, if you insist!" He loosed his fist and dropped an outraged Madowr on the hard cobbled pavement. "Away with you, vermin, and if ever you pursue Master Nickolas or any other unfortunate child again, see that I shall deal most strongly with you!" For good measure he shook a terrifyingly large mailed fist at Madowr, who blanched as white as the whey-faced Wheedle and scuttled away backwards on his hands and heels. Not once did he cast a glance at his ever-present shadow, Wheedle, who came out of his daze all at a go and sidled away like a mouse into a sewer.

Squire Daven dismounted and eyed the broken basket, then helped Nickolas dust himself off before producing a copper from his pocket.

"Here, this should buy another dozen for your lady-mother."

"But," Nickolas eyed the copper tabutz gleaming in his hand, then his old friends doubtfully, "you didn't show up just to help me, did you?"

His small face was pinched and serious as he remembered his first meeting with these two dear friends. That had been far from the sheltered valley that was home to the village of Caristoke where he lived with his family.

"Nay, Nickolas," Sir Persiflas answered gravely. "We have been to seek speech with your good king, but we thought to spend a few moments renewing acquaintance with you and your companions. Is there a place where we may speak with some measure of privacy?"

Thinking for a moment, Nickolas' brown eyes darkened, and then he brightened.

"Behind the inn, there's a way into the stable loft."

"Good. We shall await you, young master."

"Thank you for helping me," Nickolas put out his hand and Squire Daven shook it carefully.

"Any time, Nickolas. Now get you to market and home again. Time awaits no person!"

All this Joss found out later, when his little brother Nickolas came home from the market with dirty knees and torn hose, their mother exclaiming that Madowr was no better than he should be. Nickolas was awfully quiet for once, impatient to be washed and on his way again. As soon as he was clean and each of them provided with a fresh molasses cookie, their mother handed Joss a hot loaf of bread, well-wrapped and smelling like sunshine on a winter's morning.

"Take this to your Aunt Jasmin. She's been up nights nursing old Goodwife Willem."

"May I please have another cookie for Mykael?" Nickolas asked and his mother bustled about. Nothing would do but a full dozen should be tied up for their cousin and his mother.

"Supper will be late tonight, Joss. Your father's still out at Master Swinton's farm, wrestling with that mean-tempered workhorse the good master sets such store by."

With that the brothers were on their way. As soon as they were out of sight, Joss stopped and looked at Nickolas. He hadn't eaten more than a bite from his cookie.

"Out with it, Nickolas," he demanded. "What really happened on the square?"

Suddenly Nickolas grinned and he glanced about hurriedly to make sure that no one could overhear. Only Master Corwin and his new bride Azallea crossed on the far side of the square, so engrossed in one another that not even the tolling of the disaster bells would have caught their attention.

"Madowr and Wheedle knocked me down, Joss!" He protested, and then added, "but I was rescued by a knight in shining armor!"

His brother snorted.

"I ask you a simple question, Nickolas, and you go making up—."

"A knight and his faithful squire, Joss!" Nickolas cut him off, his bright eyes dancing.

Joss' mouth grew as round as his eyes in sudden comprehension.

"No!" Then, as Nickolas nodded excitedly, "Here?! Where?"

"In the stable loft at the inn. I said we'd come as quick as we could, but we have to fetch Mykael!"

Without another word, Joss sprinted towards their Aunt Jasmin's cottage, Nickolas pounding on his heels. Now he knew why Nickolas had asked for extra cookies, knowing full well that their mother wouldn't stop at just one.

The boys made short work of delivering the bread and whisked their cousin Mykael away to the stables. At ten years old, Mykael was a year younger than Joss. With his blond hair and glasses and his mixed shepherd pup, Brigady, he had been their constant companion all their lives. He stood stock-still in the lane as Nickolas told him where they were going and why.

"And Pendravyn?" he asked, naming the harmless-looking old man who had led their adventure where time ran by another clock's hands and strange and wondrous events had unfolded.

Nickolas shrugged. Brigady yipped once, and the boys were off.

Cailie pushed the damp hair back from her forehead and got to her feet. Leaving her bucket and scrub brush for the moment, she stood at the half-opened door of Maily's Cottage and leaned on the sill. The fresh air revived her and she sighed. The village green was quiet this time of day. Cailie sighed again. How could everything be unchanged with Grandmother Maily gone? Her grandmother had died recently after a long illness. The old woman had lived a long and happy life, and she was sorely missed by her family. Perhaps more so by Cailie than any of her other grandchildren, for Cailie had never married and had no home, no husband or children to fill her hours. She shook her head. Standing around feeling sorry for herself was not getting her work done. Grandfather Walker had decided that he could not look after Maily's Cottage alone, but Cailie thought he could not bear to live there without his sweet wife. He had gone south to the village of Portsall to live with his youngest daughter, Catrin, herself recently widowed with a brood of five all under the age of ten to look after. Maily's Cottage was to be rented, and Cailie had volunteered to make it ready for the first tenants.

Another sigh escaped her. It had crossed her mind to ask her grandfather if she might have the use of the cottage. But with Aunt Catrin recently widowed, the income from the rental of Maily's Cottage would allow her aunt to care for her children and her father. Heaven knew, Maily's Cottage was not big enough for Catrin's young family. Then her gaze sharpened at the sight of a knight and his squire crossing the square. For a moment, her heart caught in her throat, then she let out her breath as they headed toward Caristoke's only inn. Just passing through. The broad fertile valleys that held Caristoke and its neighboring towns and villages were peaceful, the land of Camaria secured by a strong and just king for decades now.

The wind picked up, a cold breeze bringing bumps to her arms. Cailie shivered and reached to close the half door to the cottage. Taking up her brush, she scrubbed the floor with renewed vigor, but the sight of the knight and his squire stayed with her as she worked. The kingdom might be quiet, but she knew only too well that trouble often walked abroad in the lands of the other members of the Five Kingdoms—in the mountain fastnesses of Draemar, in the far desert kingdom of Skören, in the southern plains of Bulwar, and in the coastal kingdom of Ithnan-Almara. Let the king of Camaria deal with anything that might threaten this land. Yet, uneasiness pricked at her back, and it was only with an effort that she turned her mind to other matters. Without a fire to warm it, the cottage was bone-chilling cold. She would be glad to finish up and return to her parents' farm.

Mykael greeted Sir Persiflas, Squire Daven, Rex the warhorse, and Hesperius the mule with equal measures of enthusiasm. Sir Persiflas accepted a cookie with a ponderous grace, Squire Daven biting into his with alacrity. For a moment they sat in silence, and then the knight shifted on his straw seat.

"Would that we met under happier circumstances, my young companions."

"The Chotil?" Joss interrupted anxiously, thinking of their quest to regain that mysteriously wrought cylinder. It was that which had led them to the knight and squire and to the wizard Pendravyn and his companion, the witch Merys.

"Nay," Squire Daven stirred. "That lies undisturbed."

The knight nodded, and then cleared his throat.

"We thought to warn you three good comrades. Know this, a cold wind whines in the mountains of Jashtar," he told the boys and a crooked shiver went up Joss' spine. Nickolas and Mykael inched closer to him.

Brigady thumped her tail and crept after her master.

"The Jashtar Mountains lie far to the north of the Hofen Forests, below the Snowfell Taiga, at the edge of darkness. The winds have swept down early from those mountains, out of the Snowfell, through the Hofen and onto the plains and gentle foothills. The last fruits have frozen in the orchards and vineyards.

"The winds keen at midnight, so that sleeping souls toss and turn uneasily, and the timid wake with fear."

"Doesn't winter come to the mountains," Mykael piped up, "like it comes to Caristoke?"

"Aye, winter comes," Sir Persiflas agreed, "but not with a cruel sneer and a colder touch. Where this wind walks, all in its path is blighted."

Crisp sunshine slanted long bars of light across the straw where they sat. Joss stretched his toes into that flowing warmth and pondered the knight's words.

"Why?"

The half-formed thought escaped him. He glanced from Sir Persiflas to his squire. "Why has this evil wind come down from the mountains to plague the world?" And, a whisper of foreknowledge prickled at the back of his neck, would it reach out to touch his own village?

Sir Persiflas heaved a lofty sigh; below them Rex caught the tone of his master's feelings and blew disquietedly. Mykael snapped a straw in half and bent to pull Brigady close, as if he too felt a sudden need for warmth. Squire Daven sat up straighter, little worry lines showing about his usually merry blue eyes.

"High in the Jashtar Mountains lie the crumbling, tumbled walls of an ancient ruined city. In times immemorial the high valleys and plains were home to a people so old no one now remembers who they were. But in the depths of the city there exists the remains of a crenellated walled tower. Only the round base of Za'Matl—so the tower is called—still rises, broken and ragged, out of the wreckage of the city." Sir Persiflas wiped a hand across his brow and smoothed his dark hair before continuing.

"A wind howls out of the depths of that ruined tower, or so the legends have always told, loosing the anger of its once-inhabitants upon the long-dead city. Now that wind stirs far beyond the tower, far beyond the Jashtar. On it comes—like a single-minded creature searching the land."

"Searching for what?" Nickolas asked in a worried voice.

Squire Daven and Sir Persiflas exchanged a glance. The squire shrugged slightly and the knight replied slowly.

"Legend has it that the people of Za'Matl—named after the city—had a sister-city that lay far to the south. In the unknown and terrible events that led to the destruction of their cities, it is said that the spirit of the Za'Matl rested in the heart of Ka'ma-atl, the southern city.

"That spirit sleeps on, so our legends say, for thousands and thousands of years—until the day when *'The Barque of Justice shall sail the Holy River, the Crossed Swords of Avat'ar held above the Alabine Goblet as the reborn child of Za'Matl drinks!'*"

Another silence fell as Joss drew closer to his little brother, suddenly grateful for his presence. Once more their cousin raised his head and faced their companions.

"Has that day come, then?" he asked quietly, pushing at his nose with the back of his hand.

"Not yet, young Mykael, but Pendravyn has learned that Khasil, a shaman of the Cherdir horsemen who roam the mountain valleys of the Jashtar Mountains, has left his usual haunts on the western slopes of the Jashtar and goes before the wind. He has made himself high shaman among the Cherdir and seeks to fulfill the prophecy." The knight's features were grim as he looked at his squire, and in that moment Joss saw how desperately weary both men were. How could even a knight stand against ancient prophecies? Yet, he heard his own voice asking his friends.

"What can we do to help you?"

The faintest of smiles briefly lit Squire Daven's tired eyes.

"Only this, Joss, stout-heart. Watch. Watch who comes traveling through Caristoke. Listen to the wind and the sounds of approaching winter. If all is not as it should be, then Pendravyn must know. For it may be that gentle Camaria and its towns and villages will be touched by the same dark foreboding that threatens the northern lands."

"How will we be able to contact Pendravyn?" Nickolas asked.

"Seek and ye shall find," was all the answer the knight would make. "Pendravyn will know if there is need."

Mykael caught his older cousin's eye and together they looked at Nickolas, whose lower lip stuck out as he thought hard about the story he'd heard. His quick eyes flitted up to meet Joss'. How could they think to involve him? Yet, the same determination and sheer stubbornness that gripped his brother and cousin showed in the set of Nickolas' features, and Joss knew that it would be useless to argue with him. Besides, he told himself uneasily, they wouldn't be doing anything dangerous this time.

"We'll do it," he announced.

"Aye, m'lad, we never doubted that your hearts are as strong and willing as ever," the knight nodded as if formally accepting the boys' help.

"But," Squire Daven cautioned, his face earnest, all humor contained, "watch carefully. That is all Pendravyn would ask of you. No need for anything more."

Yet. As clearly as if he spoke the word, it rang in Joss' head. Anything that could worry Pendravyn had to be enormously important.

"Then Pendravyn is trying to stop this Khasil?" Mykael asked.

"Even as we speak," Sir Persiflas rejoined. "And with your sharp eyes and ears alert here, you three who served so well in another time and place, perhaps we'll add some small bit of knowledge for his aid."

"You can count on us," Nickolas affirmed with a little nod, for all the world like his father before the villagers.

"We must pass on," Squire Daven reported, stretching his shoulders with a regretful grimace. "There are others we must visit before we rejoin Pendravyn. May you be safe from all harm until we meet once more!"

"Hear, hear!" his knight agreed.

The three boys followed as the knight and squire led Rex and Hesperius quietly down the alley and out to the edge of the village. The squire looked long at the winding, cobbled streets of Caristoke, then roused himself and flashed that heart-warming grin at them as he helped the knight mount the warhorse.

Waving until they were out of sight, Joss, Nickolas, and Mykael walked down the quiet streets of Caristoke to home and their suppers. The sight of the tidy village laid out before them filled Joss' eyes with sudden tears. The well-kept shops, his father's forge, the common kirk with its oak-lined cemetery and the larger cathedral with its abbey of clerics—these were part of his life—the borders of good folk, caring folk, who worked hard and prayed and laughed and mourned together. It was unthinkable that some ancient, otherworldly prophecy could reach out to blight their cheerful, prosperous existence.

Furtively wiping at his eyes, he took in the solemn expressions of his companions and saw that they must share his fears. Picking up a stick, he shinned it along the packed dirt surface of the alley. Brigady leapt after it with a shrill yip-yip-yip and the heavy mood was broken. Shouting, Mykael and Nickolas raced after the pup. Following more slowly, Joss felt the cold breeze of late autumn slide down the back of his neck and prayed fervently that it was nothing more.

The Cherdir

Smoke drifted in dark spirals from the smudge pots that flanked the tent flap of the high shaman's tent. The flap was drawn back, but the clan members kept to their own tent fires, well back from that of Khasil. Only Cheruk, the son of the chief, Cherdir, watched that opening with the yellow eyes of a hawk, missing nothing.

Within the center tent, Khasil's black braids swung about his face as he intoned the prayers of power.

"*'È-o-tay-'*" each line began the same: 'Hear me, o sister!' Khasil could not have said how he knew this, for the language of his prayers had not been spoken in his world for long ages. Yet the words slid from his tongue as though he had been born with them, and a part of his mind listened and marveled that it should be so, for him and him alone out of all the people of the clans.

Two months' ago, he had left his clan to undertake a spirit-mission. For two and a half decades, he had used his skills as healer and dreamer to guide his Cherdir clan, only to find that more often than not, the clan chief nodded at his words of counsel, before turning instead to old Ashdir, or worse yet, to Ashdir's apprentice, Mahkuk. Ashdir was ancient, approaching his eighth decade, and walked with a twisted hip—the result of a spirit quest undertaken as a young man. It did not affect his riding skills, however, although he had no longer ridden as warrior once he became shaman.

Twice Khasil had taken offerings to Ashdir, submitting himself to his elder as apprentice. Twice Ashdir had refused him. But his dream-visions would not be stopped by the old man's refusal, and Khasil had seen Ashdir for what he was—a charlatan, one who enjoyed the prestige of his position as clan shaman and would not willingly relinquish his false power even when he, Khasil, so clearly was meant to take up his place on the old man's death. Instead, Ashdir had accepted a callow youth—the boy Mahkuk—as his worthy successor. Bah! A boy filled with the old man's tales of power and prestige, but not truly called to serve his clan. So Khasil had decided to undertake a spirit quest before the annual in-gathering of all the clans. Then he would go before the great clan-chief of all the Cherdir, who bore the name of his people, and prove that he, Khasil, was truly worthy to become his clan's shaman.

For twelve days and nights he had wandered north of his clan, until his dreams had led him into the ruins of the ancient city of Za'Matl. Stumbling hungry and half-fevered through the ruined streets, he'd crawled at last into a sheltered spot—the remnants of a small courtyard—and huddled there against a carved stone block. To his amazement, the block had slid open, revealing a wondrous object within. An offering to fulfill his spirit-quest! He had taken it up boldly and the shock of its cold touch had nearly been the end of him, but he prostrated himself and prayed to the spirits to let him be their earthly vassal and to set him forth upon his path. And the coldness had considered him worthy and had withdrawn its death grip upon his body and soul.

He had returned to the Cherdir and begged audience with the clan-chief and then, while the chief of the Cherdir clans lay insensate from the power of the holy object, Khasil had taken from the man the clan-chief's symbol of power. In that moment, he—Khasil—had become the leader of the clans. They followed him now because he told the clan-chief what to say to his people and his people obeyed, as the Cherdir had always done.

Prayers ended, Khasil raised his head. At the movement, two silent figures moved out of the shadows to serve the shaman his supper of fresh saddle cheese, flat bread, and a flagon of wine. Outside, Cheruk's eyes narrowed as those who served Khasil stepped back into the shadows. Although the chief's son could not see their faces, his heart thumped against his chest as he thought of Nima and Chella, his younger sister and his uncle's daughter. In all the stories of the clans of the Cherdir, none had ever told a tale the likes of which had befallen his people since the day Khasil had stumbled from the ancient ruins of Za'Matl. From that day forward, it had been Khasil who directed the clans' movements, the council decisions, the warriors. It was Khasil who had chosen two maidens to ride behind him and serve him night and day. Cheruk's fingers closed about his *kerdun*, his little dagger, and then he willed them to relax their hold. As long as Nima and Chella remained within reach of the high shaman, he could do nothing but watch and wait his chance to free them. In the meantime, he strove to learn the source of Khasil's sudden power over the clans of the Cherdir.

CHAPTER TWO

Caristoke

Looking up, Joss surveyed his grandmother's keeping room from behind the book he was reading as Aunt Cailie moved about the room, gathering up empty mugs. Grandmother Charles' needle flicked like a current of light in and out of the quilt on the frame before her. Uncle Johan sat before the fire with Mykael, playing at draughts while Nickolas studied their moves with great concentration, his mug of spiced cider warming his hands. Joss' father nodded and dozed in his chair. At the far end of the keeping room, his aunts Sarina and Jasmin were gathered in a knot with his mother. Streams of giggles erupted from the group at the faces his grandfather pulled for James and Justin, the two-year-old twins that belonged to Uncle Trevor and Aunt Almeda.

In and out, in and out, his grandmother's needle flashed in arcs as she quilted fans and flowers and ribbons. Glancing up, she caught her eldest grandson's eye on her and smiled absently, her attention far away. Book forgotten in his lap, Joss looked round at a grunt from his Uncle Trevor as he shifted his newest son, Daniel, from his lap to his shoulder. Like a child charmed, Daniel's mouth curved sweetly into a smile even as he slept.

Behind Joss, his aunts broke and shifted as their brothers, his uncles Jessop and Martin, came in from the barn, having seen to the livestock for the night.

Some thin, unraveling thread of unease worried at Joss. Time and time again his eyes lifted from the unseen pages of his book to the family members who were settled about him. Once his glance caught James and Justin, sturdy and blond, building with worn wooden blocks at his Aunt Almeda's feet. Their father rose and tucked a sleepy Daniel into the cradle at hearthside. Impatiently, Joss turned his attention back to his book, only to catch himself, moments later, staring at the cradle. A log burned through, dropping on the grate. Nickolas jumped and whirled—not towards the sound, but towards the cradle where Daniel whimpered and caught his breath on a half-cry. Gently Nickolas set the cradle to rock and the baby sighed, his cry subsiding as he slept on. Joss frowned; usually Nickolas ignored the baby, who—Nickolas often protested—received far too much attention when he could not even walk or talk or play games. From either side of the gleaming ashwood cradle, twin blond heads bobbed briefly as two pairs of brown eyes surveyed the sleeping infant. Apparently satisfied, James climbed into his father's lap while Justin lay on the floor beside Grandmother Charles, stealing a pillow from his grandfather's chair. Only Aunt Cailie seemed to share his restlessness, for she did not sit with her sisters, but went in and out of the room on one errand after another, or stood for long moments at the window staring outside into the darkness. When she came away from the window at last, she hugged herself tightly, as if cold to the marrow.

As a huge yawn escaped him, at last Joss gave up the fight and put his book away. Outside the snow still fell, blanketing the drifts with yet more of the huge powdery flakes that had begun falling a day and a night before. The family had drawn together at his grandparents' farm to help look after his grandparents.

"Joss," his mother spoke quietly beside him, "it's time you went up to bed. Put away your book and give Grandmother and Grandfather a kiss while I round up Nickolas."

For once Joss did as he was bid without a protest. Nickolas grumbled under his breath, but gave in much more quickly than was his custom as Aunt Jasmin was steering Mykael about for his own round of good-nights. Once snug in the loft above the keeping room, the three older boys always whispered stories to one another before the grown-ups sorted themselves out. This night, however, it seemed the boys slept even as the last good-nights tumbled from their lips.

Awakening to complete and utter darkness, Joss lay still for a long moment until it dawned on him that no cheerful breakfast bustle reached his ears—no sound of his grandfather stamping the snow from his feet or his grandmother poking up the fire. No smells of fresh biscuits or hot coffee. No laughter as Aunt Cailie fed Sadie the cat and set the table. The silent, thick darkness of deep night surrounded him. Faintly, from below, the mantle clock sounded. Once, twice it tolled the hour. Then, more faintly yet, the merest whisper of sound reached him. A muted, rhythmic thump-thump-thump.

Without understanding what drove him, Joss sat up as carefully as he could, but even as he did, Mykael's pitched whisper reached him.

"Wait for me, Joss."

"Sh-h-h!" his cousin cautioned, rolling out of bed.

"Wait, Mykael!"

Nickolas, awake, followed Mykael as the three boys eased their way step by step down the wide planked stairwell to the keeping room below. The well-banked fire shed a soft light across the room as they stood for a moment at the foot of the stairs. On a mattress stuffed with goose feathers near the fire, Uncle Trevor and Aunt Almeda lay unmoving, sleeping soundly. Between them, two smaller bundled figures marked James and Justin. On the other side of the hearth, near the cradle, Joss' mother shifted under her blankets, but neither she nor his father woke.

There, at the foot of the cradle, lay Brigady, her tail thump, thump, thumping against the gleaming ashwood. A low-throated whine greeted the boys, although she made no move to come to them. Together the three boys slipped past the sleeping mounds about them to Brigady's side. Apologetically, she gave a nervous lick to Mykael's face, then looked over her shoulder and whined once more.

Unaccountably, his heart beating faster and faster, Joss leaned over the cradle, Nickolas at his elbow, and Mykael opposite them. Secure within, flat on his back, his face turned toward them, Daniel slept. The steady rise and fall of his breath was evident even in the dim light of the banked night fire. Yet, even thus reassured, Joss found himself stroking the tiny fist curled closest to him. The baby's skin was warm and soft. Behind Joss, Nickolas let out his breath on a short, quickly stifled sigh, while across the cradle Mykael frowned, straightened Daniel's blanket, and then stepped around to pat Brigady on the head. As the boys trooped quietly back up the stairs, the soft thumping of the dog's tail resumed. Joss thought he heard her whine once more as he crawled under the covers without another word spoken between the boys.

Cailie lay curled in a knot beneath her covers, shivering with cold. She could not get warm, in spite of her heavy woolen nightgown, two pairs of bedsocks, and extra blankets piled on her bed. Even the cat, Sadie, pressed close against her back, could not warm her. Dark shadows ringed her eyes and her clothes hung loosely on her frame where the weight had begun to fall away. Her parents exchanged looks of concern when they thought she wasn't watching, and she'd heard her father murmur to her mother, 'The child is taking Maily's loss hard.' Oh yes, she missed her grandmother fiercely, but this cold that had invaded her body had not come from grief. One hand crept out from the covers to clasp her other hand

and stroke the ring she always wore. Its silver
rose bloomed upon her finger, a gift from her
grandmother. Now the ring gave off the tiniest
whiff of rose blossom scent. Cailie breathed it
deeply, like one inhaling medicinal vapors, and
pulled her blankets closer.

This coldness had come upon her with the
first gusts of the north wind. She had no
cough, no fever, only this coldness that was
filling her up inside. It would not stop until it
had eaten her away from the inside out. The
rose too was affected, for its scent came fainter
and fainter as the days wore on. The wren, too.
She thought of the pewter wren talisman she
carried in her pocket. It lay cold to the touch
these days, and no amount of blowing on it or
holding it in her palm could warm it. Evil was
afoot in the world again, and it had reached
out to touch her.

At night, she slept little, for her slumber
was interrupted by vivid snatches of dreams.
These sometimes frightened her, but at other
times, she yearned to stay asleep forever and
pull back the veil of sleep to uncover some
truth that seemed to be hidden from her
waking mind. She could not divine the source
of the coldness, and it was clear that she could
not expect help from the wren or the rose,
those talismans that had aided her in times

past. She lay huddled in her bed and thought of the strain that had begun to creep into the faces of her parents. They feared losing her, but not nearly as much as she feared seeing this coldness spread to those she loved. So far, it seemed to her that she was the only one among family or village folk so afflicted.

The thought came into her mind then, the idea of leaving her home and making a pilgrimage to Wolverness Abbey. There was a house of holy sisters at Wolverness, which lay some distance to the north in the next valley. If she went there, perhaps she would draw the coldness with her. The holy sisters would have prayer to protect them. At least there, her parents would not have to watch her fade away.

Pulling the straps of the sled tighter, Joss hauled his twin cousins up the short slope by the miller's pond, Mykael pushing behind while Nickolas ran ahead. The sharp winter storm that had come early to Caristoke had left enough snow for sledding and snow forts and other winter games. School was let out early so that the older children could help clear paths to livestock and the streets within the village itself. Joss' father and uncles had gone with the miller's eldest sons to clear a way to the

Widow Grintuk's cottage, leaving Aunt Almeda and Daniel with Joss' mother.

Hot toasted bread with sweet butter and jam and mugs of sweetened cocoa awaited the older boys as they brought the chattering twins home. Joss' mother bustled forward to help the little boys out of their woolens while he, his cousin Mykael, and his brother hung up caps and coats and mufflers and mittens. Daniel sat supported on his mother's lap. Brigady, Joss noticed, sat at her feet. The dog whined once as he stooped to scratch her under the chin.

"You missed a fine time, old girl. What's got into you, anyway?" he murmured. Looking up to the baby, she licked his hand and whined again. Shrugging, Joss patted Daniel's arm and straightened as his mother handed him a mug of steaming cocoa.

Two days later the snow was gone, washed away by a steadily falling rain that came lightly out of the west and showed no sign of abating, night or day. Thick, dull gray clouds hung over the valley in which the village nestled. Only a vague outline of Glen Crawney Mountain could be seen. Two more days passed, as gray and dreary as the two gone before. The good village folk mumbled and grumbled about the persistent, clinging dampness, their aching bones, the puddles filling the streets and alleys. At last it was the Sabbath and the whole village came together in their houses of worship, where prayers were offered and pleas were sung. And it seemed, come Monday, that an answer had been tendered when a pallid ray of light broke through the clouds. By afternoon, one could even see one's shadow again, and by evening, the sun lowered its red disk edge below the clearing clouds to a chorus of cheers.

Holding his face to the sun, Nickolas sighed happily and left the window long enough to help himself to another piece of Grandmother Charles' fudge, bursting with black walnuts the boys had helped her gather, crack, and store. Mykael sighed, his own piece of candy untouched before him.

"I mean it, Joss," he repeated, "I'm giving Brigady away."

"To whom?" his cousin asked, his eyes widening before he added, "and why?"

"To Uncle Trevor," Mykael replied and jutted his lips together the way he did when his mind was made up about a matter. "Because she keeps running away to his house. I don't think she likes me anymore."

""That's crazy, Mykael!" Nickolas told him. "Of course she likes you! You're her master!"

"Then why does she run away?" he asked.

Joss had to admit that Mykael had a point. An idea came to him.

"Maybe she's just lonely." His cousin's face lit up as he waited for Joss to continue. "You go to school all day, right?" Mykael nodded. "And Aunt Jasmin is in and out all day long, seeing to the villagers who are sick or hurt. So—."

"So," Nickolas interrupted, "no one is home to keep Brigady company."

"And she goes over to Uncle Trevor's to play with James and Justin."

Mykael's features fell and he shook his head.

"Well, it makes sense to me," Joss defended his idea.

"Sure it would," Mykael agreed, "except for one thing, Joss. I always find her in the house, wherever Daniel is."

Taken aback, Joss stared at the other boy, puzzled. Nickolas looked from one of them to the other.

"But Daniel's just a baby." He made it sound as if it were a dreaded disease. "He can't run or play or do anything yet."

"I know," Mykael shrugged. "Who knows? I guess I'll have to let them keep her."

The three boys chewed in silence as they thought this over.

"Maybe," Joss offered a new idea, "you could loan her to Daniel for a while, and then she'd find out soon enough that babies don't make good owners."

Mykael eyed the candy in his hand for a long moment. The way his eyes blinked rapidly, his cousin could tell he was trying hard not to cry. What was the matter with that dumb dog? Mykael loved that pup and she loved him. Or, she had. Why had she suddenly attached herself to Daniel? It made no sense at all.

"Maybe if you help me," Mykael spoke at length, his voice low and dejected, "the three of us can get her to come home."

For the next week, after classes were over, his cousins helped Mykael in his attempts to cajole his dog back home. Games of fetch and catch left her whimpering, her eyes rolling from the door of their uncle's house to where the boys played outside, then back inside. But, she would not budge. Aunt Jasmin suggested perhaps the little dog was growing up and wanted to be a mother.

"Yeah, Mykael," Nickolas reminded his cousin, "remember in the summer when she stole the old mother cat's kittens from the loft and hid them in a basket?"

His eyes thoughtful, Mykael nodded in agreement.

"Maybe."

"She seems awfully glad to see you when we visit." That was true, except she could not be coaxed into leaving. Better think of something else to take his mind off Brigady.

"Listen, Mykael, let's ask our mothers if we can go out to the farm in the morning. We can hurry with our chores, and then we can ask Grandfather what he thinks."

"Sure," Nickolas piped up, "Grandfather knows all about dogs."

Mykael nodded eagerly.

"I'm sure Mother will let me go. She wants to send Grandmother Charles more tea for her headaches."

"And," Joss added as the thought occurred to him, "we can climb up Clegnar's Steps on the way back."

His cousin's eyes brightened at that idea. Clegnar's Steps were a perfect series of huge blocks of stones set above a ridge, providing one of the best views of the valley this side of Glen Crawney Mountain. It was one of Mykael's favorite places.

The Cherdir

Cheruk skirted the edges of the clan fires. The sun had yet to climb above the horizon, and the Cherdir slept in their tents. Only the night-guards were wakeful, hidden like shadows among the Cherdir's most prized possessions—their horses. Yet Cheruk's goal was not the horse herds, but the central tent pavilion that marked Khasil's resting place each night. The young man had watched that pavilion from every side, for as long as he could slip away from his duties to his father, the great clan chief who took the name of his people and who once ruled all the horse clans. Cheruk had seen how, each morning before the sun broke the horizon, Chella or Nima slipped from Khasil's pavilion to carry water within. He reached the water wagon positioned to the rear of the shaman's tent and rested his heels beside it in the deepest shadows. Resentment curled his lip—who among the Cherdir had ever set themselves so high as to command water—prized second only to the horses—to be reserved for the use of one household?

A soft rustle marked the opening of the shaman's tent and Cheruk stiffened, his eyes narrowed against the slit of light that escaped the tent flap. Without a sound, he melted further back into the darkness, for that single glimpse had revealed neither Chella nor Nima. Instead, a burly guard hefted the leather water buckets, cursing under his breath as he trod heavily on a stone. In that moment, Cheruk moved swiftly around the water wagon, away from the guard and stealthily approached the rear of the pavilion. Crouching unseen in the darkness, Cheruk strained to hear any sounds of activity within. Muffled sounds reached him, then a sharp voice barked a command. Khasil! His hand tightened on his dagger. Then another sound split the night and Cheruk rocked back on his heels in astonishment. A second wail rent the silence, and another, louder. An infant! Within the shaman's tent! Eyes wide, Cheruk shrank back from the pavilion and made his way in a daze to his father's tent.

Emira, his mother, met Cheruk's gaze over the cup of mare's milk and tea that she passed to her eldest child. Softly, so that her voice did not carry to the others within the tent, she answered the question her son had not asked.

"No, Cheruk, the child does not belong to the Cherdir. Even Khasil cannot conjure a babe from Chella or Nima. And none of the Cherdir women has given a child to him."

Defeated and relieved, Cheruk closed his eyes. He did not ask how his mother knew these things. As the first wife of the clan chief, she was mother to all the Cherdir. But from whence had the babe come? He sighed and finished his tea, a bitter taste in his mouth. One more mystery he was no nearer to solving.

Caristoke

Half way up Clegnar's Steps the three boys sat with their backs against the hot granite stone, looking down at the village below them. To the east they could see the tidy clearing that marked their grandparents' farmstead. Mykael pitched pebbles over the edge and listened with satisfaction as they pinged off the stones below. Happily Nickolas munched on a thick slice of his grandmother's cheese, disdaining bread. Joss sighed with contentment and wriggled his back more comfortably against the step.

"What a perfect day! Whoever would have thought, so close to Christintide, the weather would be almost like summer?" For there they sat with the sun blessing their faces and nothing heavier than a woolen shirt covering their arms.

"Yep," Mykael mused aloud, "it's strange, but it sure is better than being cooped up in the house."

Beside them Nickolas stopped chewing and looked at his cheese as if a mouse had crawled from within and waved to him. He turned huge brown eyes to his companions.

"Joss! Mykael!"

"What?" the two older boys chorused together. Now what? Had Nickolas forgotten his chores? Or his homework?

"Don't you remember?" Nickolas went on jiggling with impatience, pulling at Mykael's sleeve. "It is weird. Like summer, I mean." They looked at him without understanding.

"That snowstorm. Old Master Kinnen said it was a freak storm—so much snow so early."

"And then the rain," Mykael put in slowly. "All that rain just when the winter crops needed to be planted. Grandfather says all the farmers are behind now."

"And summer weather near Christintide," Joss added the obvious. "So?"

"So," Nickolas was on his knees, facing them, "Pendravyn told Sir Persiflas and Squire Daven to spread the word. If anything strange should happen, he wanted to know!"

Dumbfounded, Joss stared at his brother. Grimly, he realized that Nickolas was right. But, how to reach Pendravyn? What had the knight told them?

"He will know if there is need," Mykael recalled the squire's words.

"Come on," Joss stood up, "let's go home. You get your owl, Mykael, and you the silver piccolo, Nickolas. I'll bring my dragon. If we hold those together and think of Pendravyn, I'm sure he'll know."

Without another word or glance at the view sprawling below them, the boys trotted as swiftly as they dared back down Clegnar's Steps.

"D'you think that's why Brigady has been acting so strange, Mykael?" Nickolas huffed and puffed as the three boys hurried to the road.

"Could be," Joss answered for his cousin and pulled at Nickolas' arm. "Come on, we can talk later."

Behind the brothers, Mykael stood stock-still in the middle of the lane. Looking back, Joss ran to him and tugged at his cousin, Nickolas panting at his elbow. A look of horror transfixed his cousin's features.

"Don't worry, Mykael," Joss urged, tugging harder at his cousin's arm, "if that's her problem, Pendravyn will know what to do! Hurry up!"

Instead of moving, Mykael looked wildly from one of the brothers to the other, shaking his head as if dazed, and then he clutched at Joss' shirt front, the words tumbling from him, his voice rising higher and higher. Even then, his words took a moment to sink in.

"*Not* Brigady!" He shouted at his cousins in frustration, shaking Joss' shirtfront. "*Not* Brigady! *'The Barque of Justice shall sail upon the Holy River, the Crossed Swords of Avat'ar held above the Alabine Goblet as the reborn child of Za'Matl drinks'*!"

"*Not* Brigady!" Joss repeated numbly. "Daniel! It's Daniel! Oh, no!" Beside him Nickolas caught his breath between a sob and a cry. The boys wheeled about as one and raced back to the village.

Past Aunt Jasmin, shaking out a rug, past Joss' house, quiet in the sun, on they swept to Uncle Trevor's house where a din of mighty proportions could be heard both within and without the house. Outside, Brigady howled and sidestepped, barking in a frenzy as Aunt Almeda tried to shoo the little dog away with a broom. Catching sight of the boys, the pup hurled herself into Mykael's arms.

"She growled at Daniel, snapped at him!" Aunt Almeda fought to lower her voice, her face red and her hair escaping its bun on top of her head. "I'll not have her in the house! Take her home and keep her there!"

Inside the cottage, the noise rose to a crescendo, James and Justin wailing in a loud chorus of lamentations somewhere out of sight. Mykael ordered Brigady, calmer but still trembling, to stay as the three boys followed their Aunt Almeda inside. The twins stood side by side next to the cradle howling with all the power of their lungs, inconsolable as their mother sought to shush them.

"I'm sorry, Mykael, but they were trying to pinch Daniel and upset Brigady. I don't really think she would have hurt the baby or the boys." A heavy sigh escaped her as she picked a twin up under each arm and trundled off to quiet them.

Unheeded in the cradle, the center of this fuss slept on, oblivious to the twins, to his agitated mother, and to the three who crept close and peered silently at him. A baby slept within, no doubt of that. And no doubt whatsoever that the eyes which slitted open suddenly and the mouth which gurgled mindlessly belonged not at all to the Daniel they knew and loved. James and Justin cried not because Brigady was banished, but for the loss of their baby brother.

CHAPTER THREE

Wolverness Abbey

Astride the donkey, Cailie twisted about to wave at her parents until the road curved about the hillside and they were lost to view. Tears coursed down her cheeks, spilling onto her hand as she lifted it to wipe at them. Sensibly, her donkey ignored this outburst and plodded along without direction from Cailie. Her path took her in the opposite direction from the village of Caristoke, and she was glad enough not to have to ride through the village. Her siblings would have stopped her half-a-dozen times to argue with her. As it was, she had told her parents only the night before of her intention to travel to Wolverness Abbey. They'd had no time to enlist her sisters or brothers in argument against her. Her father had tried hard to convince her to at least let her sister Jasmin, a healing woman, try to help her sickness. But her mother, her small face pinched with fear and worry, had laid a hand on her husband's arm and stayed his furious pleading.

"Let her go," her mother told him softly. "They say the spring at Wolverness Abbey is blessed. Let Cailie make her pilgrimage.

Perhaps she will be blessed also." Then her tears fell, and she hugged her second daughter hard. "Come home to us again, sweet Cailie," she whispered in her daughter's ear.

Her father held her as if afraid his embrace would break her in two. "Sleep on this decision, Cailie," he counseled, "and if, come morning, you are still of a mind to do this, I will not deny you."

With the morning, her parents woke to find the donkey ready, a small pack at their daughter's feet as Cailie waited to say good-bye. True to his word, her father did not try to stop her, but nearly brought her to tears when he tucked a handful of coins in her pocket. Her mother slipped a packet of tea and a tin that held moist slices of sweet tea cake into her pack, alongside the hard biscuits and dried fruit Cailie had stowed there earlier.

Now Cailie dried her eyes on her sleeve and concentrated her thoughts on the journey before her. The road had wound away to a well-used track. This rose steadily, but was fairly traveled and easy work for her surefooted donkey. Even breaking to rest and eat at noonday, she should still reach the abbey before dark. At the moment she and the donkey had the track to themselves, and the hours stretched ahead of her until the noon. This trek into the hills might bring her no relief, but all the same, it felt good to be taking action. As if she rode to do battle against this coldness that threatened to take her life. Her donkey brayed loudly as though in challenge, and Cailie laughed, cheered at the thought of riding to do battle on her brave mount.

There had been, the cold thought came suddenly, sharply to her, stilling her laughter, a time when she had found herself trekking through a high mountain pass. That time she had not been alone either, but rather marched in company with warriors. A shiver ran through her and she pulled her cloak more closely to her as she recalled the long ranks of those grim-faced warriors in their dark green surcoats. Each warrior carried a longbow slung across the back, a bow as tall as the one who wielded it.

Young Cailie

Marching until her legs wobbled and her shoulders drooped, young Cailie pressed her palm against her pocket again and again on that journey that seemed as if it would go on forever. Within her jacket pocket, her pewter wren lay warm above her heart. As long as the wren's warmth did not fade, she knew that those with whom she marched were friends, not foes. How she came to be in this great company, or why, she did not know, but when, precisely, was clear enough.

She had spent the night with her grandparents in the village of Caristoke. Grandmother Maily had arisen before dawn, shaking a sleepy Cailie from her slumber. After a cold breakfast, her grandmother had marched her briskly out into the gray, chill morning to the church. Even at this hour, the great doors stood open and candles lit the hall within. Her grandmother knelt in the family pew, Cailie kneeling sleepily beside her. Quietly, the old woman bowed her white head. She was a long time at her prayers.

Knees stiff, Cailie knew better than to wriggle about. Resolutely, she kept her gaze fixed upon the altar until her head swam, images of the candles blurring before her eyes. In her pocket, the pewter wren she carried there like a secret treasure seemed to burn a hole through her shirt. Its frantic song beat at the inside of her skull as though a panicked bird was captive within and sought a way to escape. At the moment when it seemed her head would burst open, the church itself split asunder, the gray clouds roiling in upon them, obscuring the chapel, the altar, even Grandmother Maily's solid form beside her.

When the grayness cleared, she discovered herself marching in a long column of archers, the wren nestled warmly against her chest, quiet now. Where, she wondered as her frightened eyes searched the column, were Pendravyn and the lady witch Merys, in whose company she had found herself far from home once before in the midst of strange events? Even Pendarek, the witch's younger brother, would be a welcome sight.

Pendravyn

Joss stared wordlessly at his cousin and brother across the cradle. Three pairs of troubled eyes met over the infant who lay within. Who would believe that Daniel was gone? James and Justin, two years old, who had recognized and tried, by all accounts, to pinch the baby that was not Daniel? Brigady, who had known somehow that their youngest cousin was in danger? Pendravyn! As one they mouthed the wizard's name and nodded together.

A short time later, the boys crept into the garden behind Aunt Jasmin's cottage. Beside the tall privet hedge that enclosed the intermittent greenery of Aunt Jasmin's herbs, a bench provided seating. Crowding their heads close together, the boys opened their fists. Joss marveled anew at the delicate gifts bestowed upon them by Syla. An owl for Mykael, who had soared as Pendravyn's eyes to spy upon an evil wizard. A dragon for Joss, rescued by the powerful, gentle clutch of Otaghi-Ray, ruler of the Fenmarsh. A tiny piccolo whose silvery notes had burst from Nickolas' lips to hold the Tuovo cavern-dwellers entranced. These three objects linked them all to Pendravyn, the wizard with whom they had adventured.

"Now," Joss ordered, "think as hard as you can of Pendravyn."

Closing his eyes until the dragon writhed and burst into flames beneath his lids, Joss called forth blindly over and over in his mind for Pendravyn. Tense beside him, he knew that Nickolas and Mykael strove with him to reach the wizard wherever he might be. For an eternity they called, or so it felt to Joss, when at length the fire dimmed from the dragon's form and slowly the tension drained from him. His fingers went slack; he forced gritty eyelids to open. Fish-like, his eyes bulged and his mouth opened and closed several times, but no sound came forth. Then Nickolas caught his eye and grinned.

"We did it!" Mykael stirred beside Joss. For there was no doubt where they were. In the dim light as he jostled and fought his way forward with the other boys, Joss knew he'd recognize the helter-skelter tumble of Pendravyn's decrepit wagon anywhere. Except it seemed a great deal more ordered somehow. One could actually reach the shuttered window at the fore of the wagon now. Sliding the latch free, Joss pulled the small wooden door open a crack. A dark head swung towards him momentarily, and then a blue eye dropped a wink as the door was drawn shut once again.

Sir Daven! Wherever the knight and squire might be found, the old wizard would not be far away.

After the three boys had made themselves comfortable in the back of the wagon, Joss drifted off in a half-slumber as the wagon rolled on. The effort to reach Pendravyn had sapped most of his energy and he was well content to doze. No harm would come to them while the squire drove the wagon and the knight followed after with Monsterslayer. Even as the thought crossed his sleepy mind, the hard clip-clop of Rex's hooves sounded from the rear of the wagon.

The lack of motion woke Joss. Roughly he shook his companions as the back of the wagon was opened. Nickolas, Mykael, and Joss hurtled forward to meet Sir Daven, who hugged them all together, then swung Nickolas to the ground as his cousin and brother clambered down from the wagon.

"Hallo, Squire Persiflas." Joss met the squire's grave face as he tethered Rex beside the wagon. He looked more tired, if possible, than when the boys had seen him last.

"Hallo, Joss," he returned. "If you would fetch yon bucket from the wagon, I will bring water for our supper, then we shall talk."

As the squire gravely set about his self-appointed tasks, Joss helped Sir Daven start a small, smokeless fire. Mykael carried water for Imelda and Lilly, the two dainty white mares which pulled Pendravyn's wagon, while Nickolas patted Hesperius and shared half an apple the squire had given him with the mule. At length, when their bowls were emptied of the thick stew and chunks of bread which had filled them, Sir Daven heaved a sigh.

"Well, lads, let us hear your tale. We prayed that all would be well with you and that you would play no part in this uneasy season."

"Aye," the squire chimed in gloomily, "for 'tis only bad news would have made you call for Pendravyn—bad enough that he brought you to us."

"Where is Pendravyn?" Mykael interrupted.

"And Staff. I mean, Merys," Nickolas added, correcting himself. They had found the wizard accompanied by a talking staff of wood on their first adventure—a staff that had turned out to be a beautiful witch with powers equal to Pendravyn's, bespelled by an evil dogwizard.

"They come," the knight informed the boys. "Now, if you will pray tell us, what misfortune has befallen Caristoke?"

"Not Caristoke!" Joss blurted out, "but us! Daniel has been stolen!"

A look of bewilderment crossed his friends' faces.

"Daniel is our cousin," Joss was quick to explain.

"He's just a baby!" Nickolas exclaimed. "Someone has taken him away and left," he paused, searching for a word to describe what lay in the cradle now, "left *something* behind," he finished uncertainly.

"Brigady knew Daniel was in danger," Mykael reported. "She wouldn't leave his side for days, but we didn't understand. We have to get him back. He's just a baby," he repeated, his voice cracking with fear.

Sir Daven and Squire Persiflas exchanged a glance, and then the knight reached out to squeeze Mykael's shoulder.

"When was the child taken? And what exactly has been left behind? What of his parents?"

"That's the worst part," Joss answered. "They don't know that Daniel's gone. They, whoever or whatever 'they' are, have left what seems to be Daniel in his place. That is, there's a baby in the cradle that looks like Daniel, but it's not," Joss repeated, his voice firm.

"And only we three and Brigady can tell," Mykael told the knight and squire.

"And James and Justin," Nickolas pointed out. "The twins tried to pinch it," he added with satisfaction.

"I see," Sir Daven's mouth twitched at the corners, then he was serious again.

"'*the reborn child of Ma'al*'" Squire Persiflas quoted softly.

"Yes!" A chill brushed the back of Joss' neck. "We remembered the prophecy. But how are we to find Daniel and get him back?"

"Squire Persiflas and I are following Pendravyn's trail," Sir Daven explained to the boys. "We think we know where to look for the '*Barque of Justice.*' Even as we speak, Pendravyn and Merys should be on their way to our rendezvous at Partolina, a tiny port in Ithnan-Almara. Needs must we put your woes before the pair of them. P'raps they can set us a direction and a place to seek your infant cousin."

Mulling over his words, Joss' glance rested first on Nickolas, drooping with fatigue, and then on Mykael, whose tired eyes were puffy and swollen. His own head seemed stuffed with woolen rags; he could not think straight. Sir Daven was right. How could they hope to set off in search of Daniel in this strange country? Meanwhile, they might be useful to the knight and his squire in their efforts to locate the *'Barque of Justice.'*

"As you say," Joss agreed. "How far is it to this Partolina and where in the world is Ithnan-Almara?"

"I can draw you a map, my friends," Sir Daven suggested, suiting action to words with the tip of a twig. Nickolas' eyes lit up and he sat up straighter. Maps drew him like ants to sweet sap in the spring. Mykael hunched closer to the light and the squire drew a blanket around his thin shoulders.

Ithnan-Almara was a sleepy, dog-eared country that hugged the shores of the Kahma't, a twisting green river that sprawled into the ocean at Vertain-Sola. It was, Joss remembered, part of the Five Kingdoms, but try as he might, he could recall little of Master Peters' geography lessons. But for the names of places and cities and countries that rolled from Sir Daven's tongue, he might have been listening to a tale drawn from the wonders of legend and myth. The Arvold-Holt of Nansküen had hurled the first thunderbolts into the sky from the heights of the Jaskar-Kurlen Mountains. Yet Sir Daven clearly spoke of the Arvold-Holt's palisaded towns and stone-mossed cities from personal experience. The boys' eyes grew heavier with the telling and at last Squire Persiflas gently picked up a sleeping Nickolas, herding Mykael and Joss before him to the wagon.

"Sleep, little ones, while you may. Tomorrow will be soon enough to be on our way."

The familiar light of dawn broke sweetly through the vestiges of Joss' dreams when Squire Daven haled the three sleepy boys from their blankets in the wagon for an early breakfast next morning.

"We must hurry. Pendravyn has promised to meet us this side of Partolina on the bluffs overlooking the Black Fork stream."

A quick splash of cold water on their hands and faces, thick slices of ham and cheese on rough country bread and mugs of sweet tea to wash it down, and they were on their way. Crossing the border into Ithnan-Almara within the hour, the wagon followed a road that wound its way past thinning pine forests and sandstone outcrops weathered by rain and sun and wind into whimsical red shapes.

Away down a valley, at one overlook in the road, they spied a village. Or a town, Joss supposed doubtfully, that straggled its wriggling way along both shores of a waterway. Houses and farms clustered at odd intervals. A little farther downstream, another ragged stretch of similar dwellings could be seen.

"How do they know," Mykael echoed his cousin's thoughts uncannily, "where one town ends and the next one begins?"

The squire's clear laugh resounded in the crisp morning air, and Joss caught himself remembering old Pendravyn's tale of two valiant knights—all that was left when their brave king died—the two pledged to travel the world with one horse, one sword between them—to offer that sword in the service of the just, on the side of good. Squire Daven rubbed a hand over his stubbled chin, and then pointed as he explained.

"Each loose cluster of yon buildings forms a community based on a clan, or kinship ties between all the people who live there. They marry out their sons to neighboring villages, thus extending those ties to other villages."

"They are farmers," Sir Persiflas added as Rex paced sedately at the wagon's side. "Eking out a living from a poor land. P'raps it is necessary not to put too many people together in one place."

Indeed, they passed few local inhabitants as they steadily made their way towards Partolina. Those people they did see were dressed in drab olive or black trousers with shapeless tunics and cowls. Scuffed sandals or bare feet appeared to be the preferred foot coverings, and Joss shuddered as the cold wind whipped about the wagon. Only in their belts and carry-alls was there any hint of color. Vibrant oranges and reds were interwoven with turquoise and lapis and black, creating bizarre yet vivid figures and patterns.

Curious, Mykael craned his neck after one such native soul had passed with barely a nod of his head to acknowledge the passage of the wagon.

"What are those figures?" he inquired. "They don't look like any animals I've ever seen, but then. . . ." his voice trailed off uncertainly, and Joss guessed he was thinking of the saber-toothed bears, the were-fog, and other strange encounters they'd had once before when in company with Pendravyn and his friends.

"Not to worry," Squire Daven patted Nickolas' head, "those are Ithnani spirits dancing to keep ill-fortune from the wearer."

"Ithnani?" Mykael repeated dubiously.

"Yes, Mykael," the squire reported. "This country through which we are now traveling is made up of the Ithnani farmers, such as live in these straggling villages, and the Almara, hereditary rulers who live in a crumbling, sprawling palace at Vertain-Sola."

"And Partolina?" Joss ventured, "Is it Ithnani or Almara?"

"An Almarian outpost, Joss, but you shall see for yourself once we have rendezvoused with Pendravyn."

Even as they spoke, Sir Persiflas ranged ahead of Lilly and Imelda, Pendravyn's pair of white mares, on Rex. The track they followed sloped uphill and wound in and out of patches of pin oak, black maples, and beechnut trees, their leaves falling in the snatches of breeze that intermittently plagued the travelers, catching their breaths and frosting their cheeks. Well provided with cloaks and blankets by the squire, still Joss was glad enough when at last the trail widened into a clearing overlooking the deep channel where a broad placid stream joined the river. Here the wagon halted. A measure of sunshine broke through the clouds and seemed to sweep the wind away before that light, because it came no more to whistle down their necks. Stiffly, the boys climbed down from the wagon to walk their stubborn limbs into some semblance of comfort and warmth.

"What a view!" Mykael stamped his feet beside his cousin. "Look, Joss! There!" His voice rose in excitement, and they all looked where he pointed. Across the river flew a pair of great blue birds. Slowly they glided along the deep channel, majestic wings seeming to brush the banks on both sides of the river as they flew closer and closer towards the small party on the bluff above them.

"Great blue heron," the squire murmured as they passed close beneath the boys, the sun caressing the dark blue feathers into a glimmering, dazzling sight. Joss held his breath as the pair flew on and disappeared beyond the bluff on which he stood. Nickolas was speechless and Mykael whistled in admiration. Sir Persiflas nudged the squire and they moved off a little way to start a small fire.

Gathering dry twigs to feed the flames, Joss saw Nickolas drop an armful, his face lit by surprise. Jerking around, Joss breathed a sigh of relief. A tall figure in a squashed black turban and a slightly tattered robe strode out of the woods on the path above their camp. A slender woman, dark auburn hair wound in a loose knot at the nape of her neck, moved at his side. Soft curls escaped the knot to frame her face.

"Pendravyn!"

"Merys!"

The cries went up from all sides as the boys converged upon the wizard and his companion.

"My wife!" Pendravyn must have read Joss' mind again, a habit of old, the boy recalled. The wizard's azure eyes twinkled as Merys sent him an affectionate glance tinged with amusement.

"So you haven't forgotten us," Nickolas remarked, Pendravyn's arm about his shoulders as he shepherded the three boys to fireside.

"Forsooth, my little friend," Pendravyn teased, "how could we forget such a trio of stalwart apprentices?"

As they settled about the fire, a glimmer of blue caught Joss' eye when it fell from a fold of the wizard's robes. A feather floated down to nestle among the red and yellow and brown leaves that carpeted the clearing. Joss looked up to find Pendravyn's bright eyes upon him. Merys reached out to retrieve the downy feather and casually thrust it into a pocket of her robe. Mykael nudged his cousin in the side; so he too had seen.

Hastily, Pendravyn removed his mug as the hot tea scalded his mouth. Wiping his mouth with the back of a hand, he grimaced. Somehow, cooling his own cup before he drank, Joss knew the wizard's thoughts were not on the tea.

"Aye, Joss." The old man smiled tiredly, his eyes shut down and his features wrinkled, then Merys touched his arm lightly and Joss saw resolve strengthen, define that face until it held the strength and the power that had marked him as a man of special heart and talents in their first encounter.

"What, then, has befallen you, my young companions, that you have sought me out?"

For a long, long moment even the grass appeared not to rustle, the leaves without motion, the rippling of waves across the river stilled. Then the earth caught, shuddered, and time jerkily ran forward again as the boys' tale of woe ended. A swift glance passed between wizard and witch. Sir Persiflas drained the last of the tea in his mug, while the squire's curious blue eyes never left the wizard's face.

"*He* could not have done this as a simple shaman of the Cherdir," Merys stated flatly, with certainty.

"Aye," Pendravyn agreed. "But, how, then?"

"Sir?" Nickolas questioned.

The wizard tugged at his beard and his worried expression struck fear from Joss' head to his toes.

"Khasil, the high shaman of the Cherdir horse-clans, has not enough power to take yon Daniel and replace him with a simulacrum."

"A sim. . . .a simu. . . ." Mykael's raised voice parroted his brows.

"A replica," Merys explained. "Save for your association with such as Pendravyn, neither you nor any mortal being could have known the difference between the baby Daniel and the simulacrum."

"But if it wasn't Khasil," Joss burst out, "then who?" And as no one answered, he demanded, "If we don't know who, how in the world will we ever find Daniel and bring him home again?"

"I think," Pendravyn replied after a moment, "that you should hear the story of our travels now."

The Cherdir

As the Cherdir rode relentlessly towards the southern mountains which edged the vast plains of the horse clans, knowledge of the babe held by the shaman spread throughout the camps. More than once Cheruk heard whispers.

"Demon spawn," the old women spat onto the ground as they rode at the rear of the warriors.

"Slit the demon's throat and end Khasil's thrall," the boldest of his father's warriors ventured, his voice grim when Cheruk, unnoticed, sat beyond the fire and listened to the warriors' mutterings. Khasil's direction was taking them out of the mountain valleys and the plains beyond, and the Cherdir grew uneasy, although still the clan chief rode behind the shaman's retinue and said nothing to his people.

It was on another moonless night when Cheruk flattened himself beneath the water wagon and waited patiently for the stirrings of Khasil's household. At last, he was rewarded when soft footsteps approached. By the stitching on her leggings, he recognized Chella, his uncle's daughter and his age-mate sister. Cautiously, he slid his hand out and took hold of her ankle. Just so had he and his brothers and sisters played and stalked one another through the tall grass of the plains in their younger days. Chella stiffened, but did not scream.

"Cheruk! My brother," came the merest whisper as the girl hung a bucket on the water tap and opened the tap to let the water trickle out.

Cheruk palmed the narrow blade of his *kerdun*, the small knife every boy was given upon his christening on the name-taking day of his seventh birthday, in its thin sheath, and slowly, so that no sudden shadow would give him away, tucked the little knife securely down the shaft of Chella's supple boot. Above him, as his cousin set the filled bucket down, he heard the softest of whispers.

"Khasil leads the Cherdir on a quest for things of power. He has one such now, brought forth from the ruined city, and seeks others." Chella took up the second bucket.

"What of the child?" Cheruk's murmur reached no further than his cousin.

Her strained whisper could not hide her shock and fear.

"'Tis no demon child." So, even within the shaman's pavilion, the mutterings of the people had been heard. "How the babe came hence, I do not know," Chella's soft voice continued, "but he means to sacrifice the child for the power he seeks." She straightened and took the second bucket from the tap, picked up the other, and set off for the shaman's pavilion as the guard opened the tent flap for her.

Cheruk crawled away on his elbows, until he was clear of the water wagons, before darting away to his mother's tent. His eyes remained open long after he had retreated to the thin comfort of his sleeping pad. The birth of a child was a cause of great celebration among the Cherdir. Children were looked after and cosseted by all, for the Cherdir often led a hard life and too many babes never saw their name-taking day. He had seen fierce warriors tumbling like pack-mates with toddlers, a crawling baby absently picked up and held by his father during clan-meets, a young daughter cradled in a father's mounted lap as they rode to new pastures. To kill within the Cherdir was an offense punishable by banishment or death. To kill a babe? Such was unheard of among the horse clans, and only fear had caused the mutterings of demon-spawn.

CHAPTER FOUR

Wolverness Abbey

Wolverness Abbey marked the heart of a small, sheltered hollow that followed a wandering stream down from the hills. The swath of narrow bottomland that twisted along the banks of the stream held stubbled fields, the hay and barley crops already harvested and put by for winter. Closer to the abbey walls, fat brown cattle grazed on windfall fruits beneath the thick, twisted limbs of ancient apple trees. The walls, like the buildings within, were built of the honey-colored stone from local quarries.

Cailie slipped from her donkey and led him to the gates. These stood open in the slanting sunlight of early evening, pulled wide within the abbey courtyard. A bell was affixed to the wall next to the gate. The donkey paid no attention to its clanging as Cailie pulled the bell rope twice, and stepped back against her mount to wait. The coldness within her seemed to settle in her feet, weighting her in place as it slowly crept up her legs. By the time the bell was answered, she thought dully, her veins would be solidified into stone.

An arm clothed in dark blue appeared in the corner of her vision, but Cailie found that she could not turn her head to see. The donkey's rope was taken from her grasp, and then hands took hold of her forearms. The donkey trotted before her, the back of a blue-robed figure with a thick red braid hanging halfway down her back all Cailie could see of his handler. She must be marching after all, not yet frozen, although she could not feel herself walking, nor could she feel the hands that guided her. Cailie closed her eyes, but quickly forced them open, afraid they would freeze shut and she would never see again. Her downward gaze caught sight of the rose ring on her finger, and the wild panic that whirled within her calmed and settled enough that she could feel her heart beating once again. The coldness had not yet won! There was still hope as she was marched towards the abbey buildings. Marching, she had been marching that other time.

Young Cailie

The column of archers swelled in ranks as the road wound through a narrow high valley. At the sheltered north end of the valley, a formidable gray-walled castle sat atop a broken craggy mountaintop. Bright golden banners carried the symbol of a striking hawk in colors of granite. A curved stone approach led from the castle to the road Cailie traveled. At the blare of horns from the castle parapets, its great wooden gate swung out and down with a clang. The castle lord rode out alone at the head of mailed warriors with golden surcoats that shone in the cold sunlight. No cheers sent them off as rank upon rank of men rode down the curved road behind their liege lord.

Each warrior rode with his visor already pulled into place. The only sound to be heard was that of the great warhorses' hooves ringing out on stone and the jingling and clanking of mail and armor and horse bits. Now Cailie could make out the swift figures of hunting hounds coursing through the column—as large as wolves and with quick agile leaps staying out of the horses' paths. Even the hounds came silently. Cailie shivered where she stood among the archers' ranks.

At the intersection of the castle's approach road with the main road, the lord halted astride his warhorse and lifted his visor. A trio of archers at the fore of their column stepped forward to greet him. Cailie could not hear what passed between them, but the lord nodded, swung his visor down with a clang, and saluted the archers. Cailie's heart sank as those about her marched as one to the road again. Would the column never stop to rest? She could not help herself; she was so tired she could not pick up her pace. As the archers marched forward, she slipped further and further through their ranks until she straggled near the end. Behind her, she saw the nameless castle lord ride out behind the last of the archers, his liege-men falling into place behind him. It was no use; soon she would be left behind. Or worse, be trampled beneath the hooves of the mighty warhorses coming along at a steady clip behind her.

Despairingly, Cailie looked about for a place to get off the road, but here the road wound tightly through the valley with rough graveled verges that dropped down steep slopes to the river far below. The measured hoof beats of the mounted company drummed along the road behind her, and then Cailie felt herself clutched by the back of her jacket as the great lord himself scooped her up like a wayward puppy and passed her to the row of warriors who rode behind him. Down row upon row of warriors, she was passed without comment, until near the end she found herself in the ranks of those who tended to the warriors' needs, back among the supply wagons.

She was deposited with a grunt on a sturdy mountain pony behind a young man who wore leather armor and a leather visor wrought like those of the warriors who rode to battle. Her journey, it seemed, was not yet over. Cailie clung to the young rider with relief, too tired even to be embarrassed by how she had come there. Without a word, the faceless young man dipped his hand into a pouch at his side. He pulled out his hand and opened his palm to Cailie. She seized the offered barleycake with a rushing of grateful tears and devoured every morsel, stopping short of licking the last crumbs from her fingers. Then, unashamedly, she tightened her grip around her rider's waist and burrowed her head against his shoulder. The wren sang sweetly against her breast, and she dozed as the march continued through the coming of night.

Pendravyn

"Merys it was who thought of Lamath." The light glinted from Pendravyn's spectacles as he related his tale to the company gathered about him. "Lamath," he explained, "is a community of Parvani monks. Dedicated to Parvan, the god of knowledge, they live in a beehive monastery dug into the high white cliffs above the Zanolis River inland from the El'Hadi Sea."

"That's far to the south," Squire Daven interjected softly.

"For century upon century Parvani disciples have collected arcane scrolls and books on every imaginable subject."

"The reading disciples," Merys interrupted, "each choose one book or scroll for study. A lifetime is spent in the study of that one object."

A lifetime? Nickolas squirmed beside his older brother. When there was so much to learn, to read! How could anyone limit themselves in such a fashion?

"Other disciples—the searchers, who seek out forgotten works, the caretakers, whose task it is to preserve the materials, the copyists, who make the reading texts—all work together." Pendravyn continued. "Into this colony, then, I entered in hopes of finding a certain history—one that contained a reference to a certain seafaring people and their hawk-headed ships that sailed into night."

"The Hælvedden!" Mykael and Squire Daven exclaimed together.

"A legend in both our worlds," the wizard sighed softly to himself. Joss' cousin poked him.

"You remember, Joss. Granny Charles' book. When we were little, she told us the stories of Gunta-häss, the sea-raider."

"When he died," Nickolas rushed in breathlessly, "they buried him in his ship, Joss."

"And built a mound over his tomb," the squire concluded.

"Not just Gunta-häss," Joss began slowly, remembering now.

"Yes," Merys spoke beside him. "All the Hælvedden sea-chiefs were honored in just such a manner when they came to death."

"When the ships sailed into night," Mykael repeated. Almost he might have been quoting from his grandmother's book.

"Aelfris the Quiet," Pendravyn continued, "or Aelfris the Just, was one of the Hælvedden sea-chiefs who warred with the mighty, yet held a tight grip on the young bloods he ruled. He kept a terrible justice among his people—all who went astray feared the *Hælvedda*—the 'ship of justice' that Aelfris commanded. To be brought before him on that ship was to be struck by the powers on high. The truth came forth willingly or unwillingly. Retribution for the guilty was swift.

"Aelfris met his death as bravely as his forbearers and was buried among his ancestors. Of course," Pendravyn flashed a wry grin, "that was a millennia or so ago. Many sages since then have searched for Aelfris and the *Hælvedda*. And when their search was to no avail, it was wisely concluded that the tale of Aelfris sprang full-blown as a legend among those who came after the Hælvedden."

"But you don't think so," Joss guessed.

"Let's just say I have good reason to believe otherwise," Pendravyn allowed maddeningly. "One or two curiously worked copper amulets have come to light over the years."

"Years?" The squire mocked the wizard gently.

"Hmph," Pendravyn grunted testily, his white brows furrowing in annoyance, "many years—too many! Where was I? Oh yes, while I searched the libraries of Lamath, Merys traced the trail of one of those amulets."

"It seems," she joined in, her voice low and clear, "that the amulet, which bears the visage of Aelfris on one side and his ship the *Hælvedda* on the reverse, first came to light in Ap'Cha, many leagues to the east of Partolina."

So, Merys had been far to the east and Pendravyn far to the south. Hunting in two directions—as the crow—or the heron—flies! With a mental shake of the head, Joss returned his attention to the witch.

"Ap'Cha is a slovenly city that clings to the black, ragged cliffs above the Dracha River. The wind blows forever across the dry grass plains that stretch as far as the eye can see on either side of the Dracha, all the way to the foothills of the Stürm Mountains on the eastern edge of the known world.

"The houses of Ap'Cha are cut from the very earth—sod shanties with tiny windows and the black dust of the plains everywhere. Two caravan trails cross at Ap'Cha—one that follows the Dracha north and south, and one that heads west towards Lamath. The city exists because of the trade and where traders gather, strange curiosities come to light. Like the amulet of Aelfris, such as might have been worn by the people he ruled."

From the folds of her robe she pulled a round, flat copper object, pierced at one end and strung on a coarse brown cord. Perhaps as long as his little finger, Joss saw, it was made of molten copper, poured into a mold. Aelfris' features and the outline on the back were smoothed, worn from countless years of handling.

Across from Joss, Pendravyn grunted in surprise as Merys opened her fist and dropped a second amulet into Mykael's outstretched hand. Like the first, the second bore an image of Aelfris, older and bearded, the ship worked in more detail, yet, as Mykael's finger hesitantly traced the lines of that ship, Joss understood the wizard's surprise.

"The image is much sharper!" He blurted out.

"So," Pendravyn raised a brow in sudden comprehension, "this is why you came late to meet your mate, sweet Merys!"

"Sup'at Cha was eager to make a commission on the sale of another such pretty." Merys shrugged, "I could not resist following up his tale. The bearded shopkeeper was correct. Hälden-jkan, Keeper of the House of History at Ludenlathen Gate, had recently acquired this," a delicate finger gently touched the second amulet as Nickolas examined it with great interest, "from a wandering tump trader."

"A what trader?" Mykael asked.

"A tump, good Master Mykael," Sir Persiflas patiently repeated, "is a stout flat rope that goes about one's forehead to one's back and holds a cargo in place. The trader carries his goods on his back as he travels about."

"But where do they come from?" Mykael asked.

"What do they trade?" Nickolas added.

"Who knows where they come from?" Sir Persiflas shrugged. "Anywhere and everywhere. Even in Partolina, the tump traders come and go."

"I think," Merys interjected, "they originally were only those men who came from the Segriva Isles off the coast of the El'Hadi Sea. They came bearing packets of native spices and ointments. Now, some of their descendants travel the ways of this world as surefooted as their forefathers, while. . . ."

"While other men," Pendravyn interrupted with a quick flashing grin, "from other countries travel in the same fashion, selling curios or bundles of salt or finely woven sashes—whatever might be rare or useful in a new town or village."

Squire Daven chuckled to himself. Pendravyn sent a warning glance to his friend.

"Methinks," the squire explained himself, "that a tump trader may also be a useful guise for a traveler intent on trading or acquiring information, eh, Pendravyn?"

"Humph," the wizard exclaimed, shifting uncomfortably. "I've never heard such nonsense."

"But, Merys," shyly Joss touched her sleeve, "did you learn where this trader had come from, or where he found the second amulet of Aelfris?"

Her dark auburn curls shook about her face, the light bouncing among them.

"Nay, young Joss. I could delay no longer, but flew hither to Pendravyn's side." Her sly tone teased him, but Joss noticed how her hand sought and clasped the wizard's as they sat before the assembled company. He felt the shared warmth and love that overflowed from witch and wizard surrounding them and their friends.

"So," the knight cleared his throat and regarded the two amulets solemnly as the squire held them, "we have but to find this tump trader—this one wandering soul among hundreds, nay, thousands of like traders—and discover from whom he obtained the newer amulet, then we follow that trail until—!" Gloomily, he threw up his hands in despair, but the wizard eyed him sternly.

"Do not forego hope, Sir Knight! This likeness of Aelfris is near new-minted. It cannot have come to light very much time in the past, else its existence would have been known to those who watch for just such items. Therefore, it cannot have passed through very many hands."

Joss' spirits, which had plummeted as the knight gave voice to his own fears, rallied with the wizard's arguments.

"When do we start?" Three pairs of intent brown eyes regarded Pendravyn, as Mykael and Nickolas and Joss spoke in unison.

Gravely, the wizard nodded once.

"We already have," he informed them. "The trail leads through Partolina to Vertain-Sola."

At his words the members of their band rose and busied themselves with the dousing of the fire and the readying of the mounts. The wizard took the reins of Lilly and Imelda, while the knight rode to the fore of the wagon and Squire Daven ambled alongside on the cantankerous Hesperius who, at the moment, seemed content with the afternoon sunshine, the occasional snorts from Lilly, and an absentminded pat from the squire. Merys sat on the wagon bench with Joss secure between her and the wizard. Mykael and Nickolas, under protest, crowded behind their cousin from the safety of the wagon.

"The Ithnani," Pendravyn picked up the thread of his tale, "are farmers, you may have noticed," the boys nodded as he raised a brow at them, "whilst the Almara are fisher people and sea traders."

"Sea traders?!" Nickolas echoed eagerly behind his brother. The corners of Pendravyn's mouth twitched and his trim white mustache quivered.

"Yes, Nickolas, but the book troves of the Parvani suggested something quite interesting. It seems that Vertain-Sola has a long and checkered history as a seaport. Oh, at times the Almara have been in the right place at the right time, making a rich living from the trade of exotic commodities like sea-scrag eggs or Wahtani silose fabrics as filmy and glittery as a dim fog spread across the night sky.

"At other times, as now, they languish on the reputation of other generations and turn their talents to petty bickering and stealing one another's business."

Nickolas' face reflected his brother's and cousin's disappointment and Pendravyn chuckled.

"Ah, no. The Almara have never been fierce sea warriors. They'd rather retreat and live to grow wealthy and plump some other day. Yes, Mykael," the wizard threw the bespectacled boy an impish grin, "I'm coming to the Ithnani.

"So different from the Almara. The *Tome of Silius Gräs*—which, by the way, has the most interesting illustrations—"

"Pendravyn!" Merys spoke reprovingly from beside Joss. Pendravyn's blue eyes twinkled, and he pushed the black turban back further on his head, and smothered a grin.

"Yes, Merys," he returned meekly. "Where was I?"

"The Ithnani," Mykael prompted.

"Yes, the Ithnani. Silius Gräs records a scrap of legend that suggests the Ithnani came to Almara out of the west, after some tremendous disaster destroyed their homeland. Whether natural or human-made disaster, we know not what befell them, but they came from a place named the Arvaal Plains, where they had also been farmers. The disaster came forth out of the Harven Hill-lands and laid waste to their fields."

"*The Twelve Hills of Harven*," Merys quoted softly, "homeland to the twelve tribes of Ithnani. Twelve hills on the cradled floodplain of the River Stürma, far upstream from the Dracha."

"How could a floodplain have hills?" Joss asked, puzzled, thinking of the rivers at home. When the late spring rains were hard and long, the rivers overflowed their banks, spilling their floodwaters inland across the wide, flat bottomlands, pulling back at last to leave a new deposit of rich, thick mud. Mud that made for healthy, bountiful crops for Caristoke's farmers.

Merys and the wizard exchanged a glance over his head.

"The very question we asked ourselves, my lad," Pendravyn giddyapped and clicked to the white mares. "The Ithnani keep pretty much to themselves, but an old acquaintance of mine, Hizer-aban, is an Almara—"

"Quack," Merys supplied with a testiness Joss remembered well from Staff. The wizard winced.

"An Almara scholar, who knows more about the Ithnani than anyone else. Why, he's studied—"

"Drank," murmured Merys.

"Studied amongst them," Pendravyn studiously ignored that comment as well, "for years."

"Then you think," the squire suggested as he rode up beside the wagon, "that the Ithnani homeland may be the source of the Aelfris amulets Merys collected?"

"Aye," the wizard replied confidently. "We're on the right track. I can feel it in my bones. Hi-yup!" he shook out the reins once more. "Lilly, get your mind off your feedbag and get us to Vertain-Sola!"

In the silence which followed, the company rode companionably together through the hours that remained of day. As long as Pendravyn had a thread to follow, Joss reflected to himself, there was hope that they would yet find Daniel and bring him home safe again. The comforting creaking of the wagon's wheels lulled the boys to sleep. After a brief stop for a hurried supper, Pendravyn had decided they should push on towards Vertain-Sola through the night. Sir Persiflas rode ahead, ever vigilant on Rex with Monsterslayer unsheathed across his thigh.

The Cherdir

Nima knelt beside her age-sister Chella in the short grass at the water's edge. The horse clans had reached the foothills and Khasil had made camp on the banks of a stream. Chella washed the baby's linen while Nima did that of the shaman. The babe lay asleep beside them, but no one dared approach the girls with two guards standing sentinel between them and the camp.

"Such a happy baby," Nima spoke in a low voice that carried no further than her companion. "Somewhere a mother's heart is breaking. Mine would," she added in a fierce whisper, "if ever my son were stolen away."

Chella did not answer, but instead pulled Cheruk's *kerdun* free of its hiding place until just the edge of its sheath was visible. She heard the quick intake of breath from Nima and slid it smoothly back into her legging.

"At the water wagon," Chella answered the unspoken question. "We must make sure that one of us goes each time for water. Our brother's eyes have not been bound with illusion like those of our clan-father. If we can save this child, then, I think, we can stop the high shaman and save the Cherdir."

Chella wrung the last of the linen dry and placed it in the basket. It would hang to dry behind the shaman's tent. Nima picked up the child, who gave a hiccupy sigh and nestled his head beneath her chin as she cradled him closely to her. One guard swung out in front of the young women and the second fell in behind them as they escorted their charges to Khasil's pavilion. Chella swept a furtive glance across the rest of the encampment and thought she glimpsed Cheruk, taut and tall as a strung bow, slipping around his father's tent.

Inside the pavilion, the visitor who had been escorted into Khasil's presence before he sent them away to do the washing, had gone. This was a small, dark-featured man who had come before the noon-day meal, roughly clothed and dressed in loose robes that set him apart from the Cherdir. He rode as one who used a horse only as a means of getting from one point to another, not as a man who had lived among the horses and knew their worth. Chella heard one of the guards mutter "Ithnani" to the other as she and Nima left the tent, but the word meant nothing to her—whether it was the man's name or his place of origin, she had no way of knowing.

Cheruk watched Nima and Chella enter the shaman's tent, then strode away into the horse herds. His mother stood stroking the white blaze along a young mare's nose. The mare's sides bulged with her firstborn, and Emira whispered calmly to the mare.

"Be of good cheer, oh little mother, your time draws nigh. Your Cherdir mothers will not forsake you." She fed the mare a bite of oat cake from her palm. "What news, my son?"

"I have seen them both, with the child. All seem well."

His mother gave the mare a last pat and faced her son. How tall he had grown, so like his father in face and form. Not yet a warrior, not yet a man in the eyes of the Cherdir. But who else among the horse clans stood ready to restore the clan chief to his rightful role? Who else dared to brave the dark power and magic that had clothed the high shaman since he had come stumbling out of the ruins of Za'matl? Pride swelled in her heart, side by side with fear.

"We must know more," she told her son quietly as he fell in beside her, "of the thing of power he brought forth from the ruined city. Ask if this is possible for your sisters to discover."

CHAPTER FIVE

Wolverness Abbey

The window was a narrow slit high up on the honey-colored stone wall in the cell where Cailie lay. When the sun shone through the window, the stone of Wolverness Abbey brightened as if it came to life, warm and comforting. At the level of Cailie's narrow bed, her view of the room in which she lay was limited by the heavy draperies which curtained her on both sides. The foot of her bed opened onto a view of a hearth where a fire burned night and day. From the hearth, a large iron kettle hung suspended from a hook. When the sisters of Wolverness Abbey first removed her woolen robe and stripped her to her linen shift, Cailie had not even the energy to shiver, so cold did she feel within. With gentle hands, the sisters had eased her into the bed, and then one with eyes as brown and sharp as a hawk's had lifted her chin and tilted a spoonful of deep golden honey—sweet as summer and tasting of delicate herbs—down her throat. Her eyes closed upon the sisters surrounding her bed, their voices, the thought came sleepily to her, like the faraway drone of bees in a hive.

When she woke, drowsy and warm, sunlight spilled in through the window. It had all come back in a rush—the flight from Caristoke and home, arriving at the abbey with the cold sinking deeper and deeper into her very marrow. Trying to sit up, Cailie found that she could not move and panic seized her. Was this to be the end? Here at Wolverness Abbey, away from her family? A light touch pressed her head back, and Cailie looked into the gentle face of a sister. Beyond the woman at her side, others came and went. As Cailie let out her breath and craned her head, she saw that an elderly sister sat beside her on her right, beads slipping through the old woman's fingers as her lips moved in silent prayers. Another, taller sister stepped forward and once more tilted Cailie's chin up, but she closed her mouth tight and shook her head.

"No, Sister," her voice came out gruff and low. Cailie cleared her throat. "Please," her eyes met those of the sister who stood at the foot of her bed. A large gold cross was her only adornment, but she wore it with such an air of authority that told Cailie this was the person in charge in her sickroom. "I can't move." The sister at the foot of the bed nodded and spoke a few words to the woman who held the honey-gold syrup. The tall sister stepped back. "As you say, Sister Condetta."

At Sister Condetta's murmured instructions, two young novices stepped forward and pulled back the heavy blanket that covered Cailie. Her body was obscured from chest to feet with heavy hot water bottles. These were supple and fit like a second blanket, the water-filled shapes molding to her body. As she watched, the sisters at the foot of her bed brought fresh bottles to replace those that had cooled. Sister Condetta reached out and pulled Cailie's hands free of the bottles, laying them upon the bottles covering her chest. With a convulsive gesture, Cailie clasped her hands together, finding the rose ring still upon her finger. She relaxed.

Sister Condetta nodded, "Sister Amelie."

The tall sister stepped to her bedside once more and this time Cailie did not resist the offered spoonful of liquid gold.

Pendravyn

With dawn's first strong light, Mykael's elbow jabbed Joss in the back as he sat up and rubbed the sleep from his eyes. Crawling over a sleeping Nickolas, Joss pushed back the catch on the hatch at the front of the wagon and slid it open only to find the view obscured by a broad back. The back shifted slightly.

"We're coming into Vertain-Sola," the squire breathed in a low, distinct voice. "Stay inside the wagon and don't open the rear for any reason."

Uneasily, Joss eyed his cousin, who put his arm about Nickolas' shoulders as the younger boy squirmed between the older two.

"Sh-h!" Joss warned as Nickolas drew breath to speak. Bunched together, the three boys peered past Squire Persiflas. The first unexpected sight was a slender gray bazorki, a small hunting dog that had run at the feet of Sanlara the Huntress, according to a tale in their grandmother's book. The bazorki turned large black eyes upon the boys; almost it might have been a grin that curved the face of the dog as it swung its gaze back to the streets the wagon was now entering.

Craning his neck to look about, Joss saw no sign of Pendravyn or the witch. A bad-tempered Hesperius made his presence known behind them with a loud click of his teeth. Someone or something must have gotten too close. Even at this early hour the streets were crowded. Chattering figures, so different from the silent Ithnani, rolled down canopies over street-side stalls, setting out pottery and stoneware, baskets, beaded trinkets, coiled rugs, tall jars of cut flowers and pots from which steaming brews wafted spicy odors in their direction. Tump traders of all sizes and ages, browned from the elements, squatted on their heels to make their own market space or else let down their burdens for other merchants to inspect.

The squire slowed the wagon as the mass of vendors and their wares spilled into the street. The bazorki shifted on the wagon seat. A little man stuck a torch to a cold brazier before a stall hung with hanks of meat, chicken carcasses, sausages, and other things Joss could not identify. His mouth watered and he heard Nickolas' stomach rumbling, and then the little man straightened with a huge yawn and stretch, the torch thrust directly into Imelda's face. The startled mare reared, snorting with fear, and Lilly shied away from the torch. The squire rose in a half-crouch as he tried to steady the nervous team. Another hand came out of the crowd, reaching for Imelda's bridle, and then hands were everywhere as a dozen or more swarthy figures swarmed onto the wagon seat. The wagon rocked as fists thudded at the rear door. Nickolas clutched his brother's arm with alarm clear in his huge brown eyes. Mykael gulped, wordless.

Before them, the bazorki drew blood as a hand reached towards the opening where the boys crouched. Snapping, snarling, the bazorki showed why Sanlara had favored this dog above all creatures. The squire was now the center of a squirming, twisting mass. Behind the three boys, the doors groaned under a new barrage of thuds. The bazorki leapt at Mykael. His sleeve in her mouth, she half dragged him onto the seat beside her.

"Hey!" The bazorki snapped at Nickolas, all the while yipping. As if, it came to Joss, they were being driven.

"Run, Nickolas!"

Scrambling from the wagon, pushing Nickolas towards Mykael, Joss jumped, and the boys tumbled free behind the raised hackles of the fierce bazorki.

Too busy in their efforts to subdue a braying, kicking Hesperius at the rear of the wagon and the two shrill, panicked white mares at the front, as well as a lustily-brawling squire, the mob paid no heed to three small stumbling figures hastily pushing a path through the crowd which gathered about and packed the street for a better view of the goings-on.

Clutching Nickolas by the back of his shirt, Joss half-followed, half-pushed his brother into a crooked, narrow alleyway that appeared like a black slit between a perfumer's stall and a candlemaker's wares. Panting loudly in the sudden silence of the alley, Mykael dived behind the slats of a dusty barrel, dragging Nickolas, who clung to his cousin with both hands, and Joss into the musty, haphazard shadows that lay like a moldy, damp crust along the walls of the alley.

Through the broken slats of the barrel, the street and the wizard's familiar wagon were visible. Sir Daven and Pendravyn and Merys were nowhere to be seen. The flash of the bazorki's tail showed through the spokes of the wagon wheels on the far side, where the squire was fighting a losing battle, overpowered by the sheer numbers of those against him. Joss caught his breath raggedly as the squire went down heavily to his knees. Something caught the sun, and then a thousand shards of pottery splintered and sprayed in an arc as an iridescent water jar smashed over Squire Persiflas' head. Even as his heavy body slumped forward, hands of all sizes hauled him up onto the wagon seat next to a grinning, dark man who controlled the mares as they snorted and shook their heads from side to side, the whites of their eyes showing.

"What are we going to do, Joss?" Nickolas breathed in his brother's ear. His teeth almost chattering with fear and excitement, Joss stared in disbelief as the wagon began to roll away.

"There!" Mykael hissed beside them, pointing. "Look, Joss, the bazorki!"

Following the quick stab of his cousin's finger, Joss saw the sleek gray dog behind the crowd, moving along in the direction of the wizard's wagon.

"Quick!" Like three alley cats pouncing on a fish head, the boys leapt after the bazorki, pausing only long enough, while a weaver's attention was still riveted on the milling mob of laughing, jeering vendors, to filch from the weaver's supply three of the *qhahesas* or shapeless, coarse throws worn by the crowd around them. They pulled the dusty blue and gray and brown squares with a slit in the wrinkled middle over their heads as they ran. The wrinkles created a cowl-like fold of cloth that could be pulled over the head like a hood for protection from the weather, or, in the boys' case, from prying eyes. Hanging well past their knees, the *qhahesas* could have made them invisible for all the attention they received as they rushed after the trailing bazorki.

Within minutes, the heart of Vertain-Sola engulfed the three boys as the dusty turquoise and yellow painted wagon lurched along the writhing streets, the crowd lessening somewhat as they left the bazaar behind. Forced to stop at frequent intervals as the citizens of Vertain-Sola walked in the street or crossed it with little or no regard for the comings and goings of carts, riders, carriages, or wagons, the painted wagon was easily visible to the boys' straining eyes, as was the bazorki. Trying to keep to a steady pace so as not to draw unwanted attention to himself and his brother and cousin, Joss tried also to ignore the rumblings of his stomach. If he were hungry, what must Nickolas and Mykael be feeling? The older boy forced himself to concentrate on the task at hand. They had to find out where the squire was being taken, and by whom, and then see what could be done about freeing him from his captors. Where were Pendravyn and Merys and the knight?

A door sprang open beside them and a bundle of robes came sprawling onto the walk at their feet. Gasping and sputtering, a man rolled about wildly. Pulling Mykael and Nickolas out of harm's way, Joss saw the stolen wagon fast disappearing down another alleyway. Edging cautiously out into the street, Nickolas and Mykael right behind him, he took to his heels with fright.

"Oh no!" A groan escaped Joss. As dim and dusty as the other alley they'd sheltered in, this one gave no sign of Pendravyn's home on wheels. Dejectedly the trio stood in the mouth of the alley. How could they have lost the squire? And where were Merys and the knight? Nervously Joss caught himself biting at his fingernails and hastily pulled his hand from his mouth.

"Joss!" Mykael took another step into the dimness of the alley, then another, and then he was running lightly away from his cousins.

"Mykael! Come back!"

Ignoring their pleas, he ran on. With a sense of disaster, Joss grabbed Nickolas by the arm and ran after the retreating back of his cousin. As the alley narrowed and sloped uphill, Mykael's pace slowed. Suddenly he ducked aside. A moment later, Nickolas and Joss joined him. He held a finger to his lips to silence the gasp that squeezed from Joss' heaving lungs.

The bazorki looked from Nickolas to Joss, and then focused her attention on the grating that jutted over a sunken window well.

Wordlessly, Mykael pointed. Some sort of dark cloth had once covered the window let into the base of the wall, but this was now thin and tattered such that the light from a sputtering candle cast a faint glow within the jumbled cellar.

By the wan rays of the lone candle, a figure stirred and moaned on a pile of sacking. Squire Persiflas! Hope surged through Joss. The bazorki put a paw on the rusted grating and whined. Turning about in the near-darkness of the alley, Joss swept the ground before him with a hand. His fingers closed on a broken wooden barrel stave.

"Nickolas," he whispered, "keep your eyes on that cellar window and let me know if anyone comes!" The pale blur of his brother's face bobbed up and down as he nodded.

"I'll help." Mykael picked up another broken barrel stave and moved beside the older boy. "The bazorki will warn us if anybody comes along this way." The dog had already taken up a stance between the boys and the pile of boxes and crates that sheltered them from view of anyone who might pass the alley's opening onto the street beyond.

Rusted and heavy, the grate refused to budge at first. Trying not to panic, Mykael and his older cousin shifted their weight as they attempted to push their slats inch by inch beneath the grating. At last these were securely wedged in place. Together the boys pried the grating loose, and then pushed down on the ends of the barrel staves to slowly raise the grating. Nickolas, ahead of them, pushed the end of a stout crate under the edge of the grating to prop it open.

Sweating and gritty, Joss sat back to think a bit. The gray bazorki pushed past his side and stared into the cellar. Gingerly Joss retrieved his barrel slat and poked it into the well, catching the torn curtain and easing it aside.

"There's a lot of junk down there, but we should be able to climb down."

"Hey!" Nickolas exclaimed, startled as the bazorki leapt past him into the window well. A slight rustle reached their ears before the dog reappeared by the squire's side.

"Come on," Joss whispered to his companions. "You go first, Mykael, and help Nickolas down. I'll bring up the rear."

They'd go together, he'd decided in a flash as the bazorki disappeared. Whatever happened to one of them would happen to all. He wasn't going to let his brother or his cousin out of his sight if he could help it.

"Okay, Joss," Mykael's gruff whisper reached him. Joss swung himself down into the window well, taking care not to touch the crate shoring up the rusted grating.

Squire Persiflas had a knot on his forehead and the skin around one eye was looking bruised, but he wasn't bleeding and for that Joss felt relief wash over him. Mykael had already located the only door. As quickly as possible, Joss made his way to his cousin's side through an assortment of broken chairs, rickety boxes and trunks, and bulky odds and ends. Of some smoke-stained and blackened timbers, the door appeared depressingly solid and well-built. No latch showed on their side. Frowning, Joss considered their situation. That must mean that the door opened out into whatever room lay beyond the cellar. Mykael pulled at Joss' arm and inched his mouth close to the older boy's ear. Except for the small rustles they'd made climbing in, the only sounds they had heard had been their own breathing—which sounded alarmingly loud to Joss—and a host of other rustlings which registered uneasily in the back of his mind. If he'd time to think about them, he would have wondered what small creatures were hiding in the shadows cast by that solitary candle.

"Look!" Mykael breathed the words into Joss' ear. "Up there!"

Following his pointing finger, Joss made out a narrow, barred slit—more like an air vent than a window—at the top of the door. Nodding at Mykael, he pursed his lips and looked about in the near darkness for something on which to stand.

Grunting with exertion, they shifted a trunk against the door. On top of this went a box and on top of that Joss balanced precariously and strained his eyes at the grilled opening. Beyond lay a hallway lit only by a smoldering torch at the foot of a shallow set of steps that rose up into a pitch black well of darkness. No guards were visible. By pushing his face tight against the rough, cold metal bars of the grill, it was just possible to view the area immediately below him in front of the door. Nothing moved there, and, his heart sank down to his toes, no amount of effort on their part was going to move that door. A heavy plank, as solid looking as the timbers of the door itself, barred the door on the hall side.

Young Cailie

A piercing whistle roused young Cailie. She let go her rider and slipped awkwardly from the pony's back as the young man dismounted and whistled sharply again, removing his leather helm. The hounds came coursing through the milling camp to him. He reached out to Cailie and handed her the pony's reins. Thin, rawboned, his hair was the color of the earth and his eyes the color of the black rocks of the mountains. He was a good bit taller than Cailie, but not yet a grown man. She could hear his youth in his voice, its tones sounding newly minted, like her elder brother Merriwether. The thought of her brother with his tumbling black curls and ready grin brought a lump to her throat.

"An' it please you, Miss, see to our mount, then we'll see to this lot before our supper?"

She took the reins and nodded, glad to have some small task to order her mind. Animals needed tending, that task she could do.

"Cade," her companion supplied his name as he passed a brush to Cailie. They were part of a smaller encampment within the larger camp—part of those who tended the hounds and saw to their needs. To Cailie's surprise, this included brushing each hound until its coat shone. What might have been a glint of humor passed across Cade's face, but his tone was mild when he spoke again.

"Ay, Miss—"

"Cailie, I'm Cailie," she told him quickly, blushing.

"Ay, Miss Cailie," he continued softly, "a good brushing lets you find any cut or scrape, any bruise, any tick or such that might have lodged itself below the coat. These hounds are warrior-bred. They'll fight to the death for their master and many's the warrior who owes his life to his hound."

Brushing the hound at her feet, Cailie felt the coat carefully with her fingers as she worked. The hound sat patiently, every so often turning its head to watch Cailie with great dark eyes, its tongue lolling out of its mouth to give her a quick lick. Finished with his own hound, Cade nodded to a burly giant of a man who stood at rest nearby.

"To me," the man commanded and the hounds quivered. "We go." Man and hounds bounded away towards the main encampment. Cade watched them go, then dug in his bag and brought out two bowls.

"Come," he nodded at the fire. "Herrell's generous with his stew."

With the hounds groomed, fed, and gone back to their masters, young Cailie sat with Cade at the outer circle of Herrell's fire as night came down.

"Cade?" Cailie voice was hesitant, carrying no further than her companion. His head swung in her direction. "Where do we march? And why?" 'And of what use am I,' Cailie thought with bewilderment, although she did not speak that thought aloud, 'to an army marching to war?'

Cade's dark eyes gleamed in the firelight as he tossed the dregs of his tea into the fire.

"We march to Draemar in the fastness of the Jashtar Mountains." He regarded her steadily for another moment. "Alaric, the king's cousin, stole away with his father's sword and slew the monks of Rebehan. There did he take a great treasure." Cade dropped his voice. "With his kin's blessing, the king ordered his knights after Alaric, then did Alaric join forces with Bakshir."

Cailie shivered and nodded. The names meant nothing to her. Her village of Caristoke was far from the Jashtar Mountains, but men had gone to war over less than stolen treasure. Cade opened the pack beside him and rummaged inside, pulling out two blankets. After passing one to Cailie and wrapping one about his shoulders, he continued his tale.

"Bakshir is a drummer—one who summons the spirits for guidance. Most drummers serve their people in a village or a lord's hold—or even the king himself." Cade shifted and his voice deepened. "Bakshir serves only himself. He summons spirits to gain power for himself. Alaric and Bakshir are besieged at the citadel of Wenshar. The drummer has called upon strong spirits to hold off the king's forces. We march to the king's aid."

A small breeze stirred the dying embers of their fire, shooting a spattering of red sparks into the night air.

"For treasure then?" Cailie shrugged her blanket closer and felt surreptitiously for her wren. Its warmth comforted her. "What kind of treasure is worth a war between kin and king?"

"A holy treasure," her companion corrected her. "One that must be rescued from the likes of Bakshir. Sleep, Miss Cailie, if you can. We ride before dawn."

Following Cade's example, Cailie rolled herself in her borrowed blanket close to the dying embers of their fire, her tired thoughts drifting. The young man's unexpected kindness lessened the ache she felt at being so far from home. Cade had not complained about being saddled with her, but had looked out for her and made her feel useful. There was something watchful about him, too, the thought stirred sleepily at the edge of consciousness as Cailie slipped towards sleep. There was something about him that reminded her of someone else, but who? Maybe her older brother, Merriwether, who looked after her and bossed her in equal measures. It was comfortable, she acknowledged to herself, but also irritating. She was no longer a child—though slender and slight of build, she had reached her sixteenth birthday with the coming of the new year.

Her mind drifted further. 'A holy treasure,' Cade had said. And calling spirits. This was a matter for kings and those others who wielded a different kind of power—like the wizard Pendravyn and the witch Merys—not for a frightened girl. Her thoughts spun looser. What kind of power would Pendarek, the witch's brother, bring to this battle? Now why had he come to mind, she wondered briefly as sleep stole upon her. He wouldn't remember her, she thought as sleep claimed her.

Across the fire, Cade heard the slow, even breaths that told him Cailie slept at last. Careful to make as little noise as possible, he stood up, walked around the fire, and draped his blanket over her still form. Herrell came to the fire then and rolled himself in his own blankets with a nod to his assistant. Cade's soft steps took him into the shadows of the trees by the houndsmen's mounts. He closed his eyes. A moment later, a dark gray hound with black markings loped out of the shadows past the tethered horses and ponies, towards the open ground beyond the camp.

The Cherdir

Long into the night, the oil lamps burned within the high shaman's tent, though none of the Cherdir came close enough to hear the endless recitations of Khasil's prayers. For prayers they must be, Chella thought, her eyes smarting from tiredness. She lay on her pallet of blankets, the babe between her and Nima. The drone of the high shaman's voice was nigh hypnotic, for he intoned the same phrases over and over again. She could make no sense of his words; his prayers were fashioned from a language none among the Cherdir had ever spoken, of that she was certain. She watched as he knelt prostrate upon the tent floor before some object he had taken from one of the chests kept by his chair. He had taken it out with his back to her and she caught no glimpse of it as he prayed unceasingly. It seemed to her that the tent was colder than it should have been since the shaman had begun his intonations, the chill seeping through the sturdy tent floor and her pallet so that her limbs ached with cold and would not warm.

Nima, she noticed, had pulled the babe into the curve of her body, as if to add her warmth to that of their blankets. The child slept through the high shaman's long vigil, his soft cheeks flushed rosy with health and long lashes sweeping his cheeks. Fair hair grew in curls about his forehead and ears and neck. And one chubby fist held tight to a fold of Nima's shirt even as he slept.

It was, she guessed, near to dawn when Khasil grew silent, replaced the object before him carefully into its case, and stood, stretching. He shifted his attention toward the corner of the tent where she lay with her age-sister and the babe. Chella closed her eyes to the merest slits. Khasil's frown smoothed away as his gaze swept the child, as if to make certain the babe had not disappeared. And as Chella watched, Khasil's features distorted into a twisted, gloating smile of triumph before he looked away and left the tent.

Chella let out her breath slowly. She had not cried since she was a little girl, but tears started in her eyes now. Whatever dark power he summoned lay where the shaman had once had a human heart, she thought. Chella moved instinctively closer to the baby. He would have to kill her first before she let him harm this child. They had her brother's *kerdun.* If need be, Khasil would feel the bite of its blade before she took her final breath.

CHAPTER SIX

Wolverness Abbey

Veiled light hung about the chamber in Wolverness Abbey where Cailie lay when she roused once more. The young sister at her side nodded as she dozed in a chair pulled close to Cailie's narrow bed. The silence of the cloister beyond her sickroom was complete and for a second Cailie wondered at this. Should there not be sounds of the sisters keeping the holy hours through the night? As she strained to hear, it seemed to her then that she could make out a soft chanting that filled her chamber like golden motes dancing on the very air. She flicked a quick glance at the sister still nodding unawares at her bedside. Now the joyous music was expanding in her mind until the part of her that was Cailie—free from her body—was aswirl with the music, and it seemed only natural to give herself up to the flow of sound and let it lead her where it would.

After a time, the pace of the music lessened and the sound faded. The sparkling light faded, too, and Cailie found herself alone in the dark. For a fleeting moment, she was afraid, and then she thought this must be what it is like, that last moment before death claims us. She would have liked to have kissed her mother and father one last time and to have made her farewells to brothers and sisters. She heaved a short sigh.

No. Cailie's awareness focused on that sigh. She had left her body in Wolverness Abbey. She, Cailie, had not loosed that sigh. Who, then? Concentrating, Cailie stilled her thoughts. There was the sound of breathing, quick breaths, as though someone else was nearby, someone agitated. As if gliding in a slow circle about the center of her consciousness, Cailie searched, and there it was.

A faint shift in the darkness, another bitter sigh. Cailie let herself be drawn to that sound and found that she was looking at a dim scene. Two young women with many dark braids knelt on a heavy red carpet. Their braids swung forward as their foreheads nearly touched the carpet before them, obscuring their features. Beyond them was a single table; a tall-backed chair was drawn up to one side of this, placed with its back to the women. A circular, footed iron basin held the dying embers of a fire which cast low shadows across the tented walls. Someone sat in that chair, for a bowl stood on the table and as she watched, an arm reached out from the chair, the hand of which dipped into the bowl and flicked its fingers at the fire.

An acrid smell assailed Cailie as smoke filled the tent. A gurgling murmur froze her thoughts. The hand rose as if to summon the women, but when the sleepy gurgle stopped, the hand reached instead towards the bowl again.

Then came a wrenching of her body and the scene swung in crazy arcs and dissolved. Her shoulders were being shaken hard; Cailie opened her eyes with a gasp to find Sister Condetta standing over her. The sister who had dozed at her side stood beside her superior, the young woman's hand covering her mouth and her eyes wide with fright.

"I'm here . . . I'm here," Cailie gasped weakly, and Sister Condetta relaxed her hold.

"Thank our Lord! The tea, Sister Ylana, now, please!"

A cup was passed to Sister Condetta, who steadied Cailie's head and tipped the fragrant brew down her throat as a pair of sharp eyes stared hard at Cailie, who felt a momentary wonder. Yes, she was here—in time and place back in her room at Wolverness Abbey. But where had she been and through whose eyes had she just witnessed that scene in the tent?

Whose bitter sigh had sounded in the darkness?

Pendravyn

Demoralized, Joss climbed down from his perch to Mykael and led the way back to Nickolas and the squire. The bazorki sat at Nickolas' side, the boy's hand absently smoothing the fur on her neck.

"Locked," Joss reported with a gulp.

"Well, we can't haul the squire out that window," Mykael observed in a gloomy whisper.

"And we have to find Imelda and Lilly and Hesperius," Nickolas chimed in, adding with a confidence his brother did not share, "Pendravyn will need his wagon when we get out of here."

Dejected, the boys huddled next to the squire while Joss tried to think what they should do. His cousin and his brother were right. They needed to get out of this room and have a look about to see if there was any chance at all of rescuing the squire, now they'd found him, along with the animals and the wagon. Something warm nudged him and he looked down to find the bazorki's grave eyes watching him. Maybe there was a way.

"Mykael," Joss sought his cousin's shoulder, tapped him, and whispered to him, "see if you can find something long and flat and strong. Nickolas, try to wake the squire up. Pat him on the cheek and talk to him while we look around."

Scrabbling in the dusty piles, Mykael struck upon a shovel with a broken handle.

"Squire Persiflas, wake up. It's me, Nickolas. Squire Persiflas!"

Nickolas' steady patter as he tried to rouse the squire continued behind them as his cousin and Joss approached the door.

"You climb up and keep watch, Mykael. I'll work on the door."

As soon as his cousin scrambled up and gave the all-clear, Joss thrust the flat blade of the shovel between the door and its frame below the slotted bar that blocked the cellar entrance. At last the blade end worked free. Sweating, he cast an eye up at Mykael, whose blond head bobbed once. No sign of the squire's jailers. A second quick glance showed Nickolas tugging at Squire Persiflas' vest. Giving his attention back to the task at hand, Joss bent all his strength upon the jagged shovel handle, hoping to pry up the wooden plank that locked them in. There! Beneath his hands, he felt the plank budge. Harder! No! Up came the handle, down went the bar! By himself, he could not lift the heavy timber free of its cradle.

Wiping the sweat from his eyes, he looked about in near panic. The squire was sitting up groggily, slumped over as Nickolas patted and tugged and pushed at his shoulder to hold him upright. Someone had to stand guard. They did not have enough hands or eyes among them. Joss gulped unsteadily, and then gasped as a lithe shadow streaked up the stacked boxes to join Mykael. The bazorki!

"All right! Good girl!" Mykael crooned, giving her head a quick pat as he hastened to the ground to lend his strength to his cousin's. With renewed effort, the two boys pushed down on the shovel handle until the bar rose inch by inch.

"Push, Mykael!" Joss whispered fiercely, but try as they might, they could not lift it free. The boys sank to the floor and struggled to quiet their ragged breaths.

"There's got to be a way out!" Joss pulled himself up. Mykael retrieved the candle and shielded its flickering glow from the grill as Joss ran his hands around the door.

"Look, Mykael! Here!" The squire's captors had bonked him on the head and left him senseless in this cellar behind that massive locked door, confident that their captive was in no shape to escape. But it was clear that no one had spent much time or effort looking after things properly. The hinges of the door were rusted, biting into the masonry blocks of the wall. Joss grabbed the shovel blade and pried the tip under one end of the bottom hinge. The shovel bit into the crumbling mortar like sand and within moments the block came free, hinge still attached. The other blocks around it were just as dilapidated and loose.

Mykael handed the candle to Nickolas, and then together he and Joss dug out enough blocks to make an opening large enough for Mykael to wriggle through. Within moments Joss heard the bar sliding free. After a cautious look up and down the dim hallway, together he and his cousin pushed the massive door open wide enough for passage into the corridor. Behind them the bazorki leapt from its look-out and followed the uneven gait of the squire, who steadied one arm across Nickolas' shoulders. Quickly, Joss moved to the squire's other side and pulled Squire Persiflas' free arm around his own shoulders. Mykael was already pushing the door shut once more, sliding the bar into place and stuffing a sack pilfered from the cellar into the hole they'd made. In the faint light of that underground corridor, the squire's captors might not notice a darker area—especially when they would be looking at the barred door of the cellar. Now there was nowhere left to go but up the flight of stone steps.

For what seemed an eternity, Nickolas and Joss struggled to guide Squire Persiflas. Ahead of them, their cousin and the bazorki peered with caution farther along the dark corridor. A flick of Mykael's hand motioned them on. The corridor gave onto several storerooms, some of the doors ajar as the small group passed. A quick peek inside showed tall rounded jars holding oils, while a hasty glance into another room revealed bales of rough cloth that gave off a musty odor. From a distance came a series of muted clinks and clanks and voices, one raised in a rumbling grumble to which a much lower pitched, gruff voice responded.

Then, from farther along, a dry, wheezing bray reached them. Hesperius! The bazorki's ears perked up. The stables must branch off directly from this dark hallway. Where Hesperius was stabled, Joss hoped, they'd find Pendravyn's white mares and the wagon. The squire's pace quickened and he straightened between the brothers. Hurrying, Mykael halted before a gloomy doorway, holding up his hand to wave the rest of his companions on slowly.

Like the owl, the thought crossed Joss' mind, his cousin once again guided them in the near darkness. Joining him, Joss peeked around the doorway and saw another shallow flight of steps. These opened into a crowded courtyard in which Pendravyn's wagon stood forlorn and abandoned. A rustle and a lonesome whicker drew Joss' eye to the opposite side of the courtyard. Four stalls open to the stable yard spilled musty straw onto the rough stone floor. In three of these, Hesperius, Lilly, and Imelda pulled against their tethers. The fourth stall stood empty save for a pile on straw in a far corner. Straining his ears, the only sounds Joss could hear were the sounds of their mounts and the occasional rumbling voices that drifted to them from farther along the passageway. Not a soul was to be seen in the neglected courtyard. Whoever had kidnapped the squire did not seem to expect trouble.

"Nickolas!" Barely raising his voice above a whisper, Joss pointed, "take the squire to the wagon and climb in. Mykael and I will hitch up the mares and grab Hesperius. And you," he pointed to the patient bazorki, "you stand guard, okay?"

Legs trembling and knees knocking, Joss stepped from the shadowed hall into the bright sunshine of the courtyard. Imelda snorted a welcome as Hesperius rolled his eyes and yanked harder at his tether. Behind the boy, the squire trod heavily at Nickolas' side. Mykael brought up the rear. As the small group advanced into the open courtyard, without warning a ray of red light shot up from the ground before Joss to well above his head. The acrid smell of burning filled the air as one after another of those red rays shot up from the ground. Whirling around, Joss saw that they were surrounded. Pillars of the menacing red light ringed them in.

"No!" Instinctively, Joss jerked Mykael's hand back when he would have touched one of those bars. Instead, Joss picked up a bent straw from the courtyard and tossed it at a red pillar. With a pop and sizzle, the charred remains of the straw crumbled on the pavement. Gulping, the boys moved closer to the squire in the center of that ring. Trapped! Who would come to see what their trap had caught?

As if in answer, a deep chuckle sounded above their heads. Shading his eyes with his hand against the glare of the sun, Joss looked up. A second-story rose above the door from which they had entered the courtyard. A row of windows stood shuttered against the noon-day heat that beat at them. All but one, that is, and from that window a short, pasty-faced man, bald and exceedingly stout, leaned both pudgy arms upon the windowsill and laughed at the sight they presented below him. With a curious gesture, he waved a hand at his captives, and the pillars drew more tightly together. Joss pulled Nickolas closer to the squire. Mykael edged beside him as they tried to keep their distance from those flaming bars.

"Tell me where your friends have hidden, little ones," called the man above them, "and perhaps I will only scorch your toes!" He slapped the windowsill and burst into raucous laughter. The pillared ring tightened once more about the boys and the squire. "The Cherdir shaman's not crazy after all! He warned us to watch for his enemies, and he'll pay handsomely for your capture." Clapping his hands together, he pointed at Joss. "I say again, tell me where your friends are hiding!"

"Let the others go," Joss shouted, "and I'll tell you anything you want!"

The fat man stopped laughing and leaned farther out the window.

"So you do know where they are! Tell me, noisome brat, or you shall all perish!"

A gray shadow flickered on the edge of Joss' sight. The bazorki! So fast did she leap from the roof of the stable to the window where the fat man leaned, that all he saw from below was a gray streak which resolved itself into the bazorki, teeth bared and snapping above the throat of her captor, her paws planted firmly on the man's chest. The force of her leap knocked him onto his broad back, teetering half out the window.

Mykael grabbed Nickolas in excitement, but no one spoke, mindful of those other voices within the dwelling.

"Call off this wolf!" The dumpy figure croaked with fear. "I shall spare your miserable hides!" he added for good measure.

"No deal," Joss called up to him. "Set us free first, if you don't want your throat ripped to shreds!" The shining white daggers of the bazorki's teeth snapped closer, made all the more frightening by the fact that the hound was completely silent in her attack. Blubbering, the man waved one arm wildly. The red pillars disappeared.

"Into the wagon!" The squire commanded, boosting Nickolas onto the wagon seat even as he spoke. Joss was already undoing the rope that tethered Lilly in her stall, Mykael fast at work on Hesperius as the squire backed Imelda into place between the wagon shafts. Above them, the bazorki never wavered. Sweat glistened on her prey's bald head as he sputtered and muttered. Even as Mykael tied Hesperius to the rear of Pendravyn's wagon, the squire wheeled it about towards the barred gates of the courtyard. Springing to unbar them, Joss saw the bazorki leap free of her perch. Immediately the man sagged into the room beyond, his voice a screeching shout.

"Halt! Halt! Guards!"

The clatter of shutters flung open reached him as Joss heaved and struggled with the heavy bar at the gates. The squire urged on the frightened mares as Hesperius brayed in indignation. A dozen of the small dark men who'd captured the squire earlier raced into the courtyard. The bar gave at last and the gates swayed open. Twisting about, Joss rammed the bar forward into the chest of the black-eyed grinning fellow reaching for him. Landing hard on the paved ground, the man gasped as the air was knocked from his lungs. Mykael swung from the rear frame of the wagon, kicking another swarthy man square in the back as he tried to mount a bucking, angry Hesperius. The man pitched off the other side of the mule, falling on his head in the stone courtyard.

Squire Persiflas put out a large hand and Joss grabbed for it, heaving himself aboard the wagon beside the squire just as Nickolas smacked a third attacker on the crown with a heavy black iron griddle hastily retrieved from the wizard's supplies. His eyes rolling up, the would-be attacker slid down the side of the wagon with a groan just as it cleared the gates. The mares bolted for freedom through the alley, the wagon careening from side to side as they rounded the corner onto a side street. A scrabbling noise reached Joss. Fearing another attack, he looked back to see his cousin pulling the bazorki into the rear of the wagon. Down the street they flew still at a breakneck speed, reaching a main thoroughfare at last. The squire slowed here, blending into the busy traffic of the street. Every now and then Joss looked back at the traffic and crowds behind them, but no one followed.

"Where are we going, Squire Persiflas?"

The squire gave a quick glance about them, wincing with the movement as if his head pained him.

"Where we were meant to go when first we arrived in this accursed town. To a safe place. You shall see in a little while."

With that the boys had to be content, for the squire gave all his attention to the crowds pushing about them from the street stalls and cross-streets. Ahead of them, a fountain spilled its flowing waters onto banks of bright red and orange and yellow flowers. Staring with longing at that cool, splashing liquid, Joss felt the wagon turn and jerked his attention away from the fountain just as the squire whipped the wagon neatly out of traffic and into a blind, dead-end alley. What now? Even as Joss opened his mouth to ask, a gate opened inward before them and the squire sent Imelda and Lilly into the gap at a trot. As the gate closed behind the wagon, a familiar turbaned figure stepped forward to greet it.

"Pendravyn!" Mykael and Nickolas exclaimed together, jumping down from the wagon. In front of them, Sir Daven steadied the mares as the squire climbed with care from his post. Joss followed more slowly, looking about him with interest. Another fountain flowed and gurgled through an arched doorway behind Pendravyn. Hesperius went as docile as the mares for once with another grinning Almarian towards a tidy stable stall. Then, from behind Joss came a low, sweet voice.

"Well, Pendravyn? Will you help me down?"

Merys!

The witch stood before the wagon seat, putting out a dainty hand as the wizard moved to assist her. A small smile played about her features. What, Joss wondered grumpily, was everyone smiling about? They'd nearly been kidnapped, then attacked, they hadn't had anything to eat all day, and he for one saw nothing funny about the situation.

"Quite right, young man!" Pendravyn clapped a hand on the young man's shoulder. "Come along, come along! Hizer-aban has food and drink awaiting us inside."

Hizer-aban was a tall thin fellow with a shock of frosty white hair perched like wings over each ear. His long sharp nose and face hid a cheery nature as he flapped his arms and set his manservant to serving platters of juicy roasted meat and cheeses and sweet fruits and, best of all, pitchers and pitchers of the lovely cold clear water that sparkled in his fountain.

When the rumbles in his stomach subsided, and even Squire Persiflas appeared to have regained his good humor, Joss put down his knife and fork.

"Where were you this morning, Master Pendravyn? And where were Sir Daven and Monsterslayer when the squire was kidnapped?"

The wizard tugged at his beard.

"A wizard's never around when he's needed, eh Joss?"

Flushing, the boy started to protest, but Pendravyn held up a hand.

"Nay, I will answer you, Joss." Taking a long pull from his mug of ale, he wiped his lips and the twinkle, it seemed, from his sea blue eyes. His face hardened and once more Joss was reminded of the power wielded by this harmless looking old man. "There are those in Vertain-Sola, my young friends, who dabble in the black arts. My face, it can be said without false modesty, is not unknown to them. So, having no wish to announce our arrival, Sir Daven and I slipped into the city by separate paths. We felt one man driving a wagon would draw no undue attention to himself."

The squire rubbed the back of his head.

"Verily," he winced as he nodded, "'twas a good-seeming plan at the time."

"But who could have known we were coming?" Nickolas turned a curious gaze upon the grown-ups.

"Ah," the wizard arched a brow at him, "an excellent question, Master Nickolas. Someone with a reason to keep us from tracing the source of those amulets."

"And now we'll never know!" Joss blurted out in frustration, for it seemed as if they were no closer now to finding Daniel than they ever were. Where was he at this moment, that bright-eyed baby whose laugh made the whole world seem happier?

Young Cailie

Stiff in every joint, Cailie rode saddle sore and exhausted behind Cade as the army marched on and swelled with new forces as it moved inexorably closer to the stronghold of Alaric and Bakshir. She and Cade had fallen into a routine, each night caring for the hunting hounds as soon as camp was pitched. As if he were always aware of where she was, in the confusion and noise and chaos of striking or setting up camp, she would look about to find Cade turning, as if a hound to the scent, unerringly in her direction. She could never find herself beyond the reach of those cool dark eyes, and it was a small annoyance that pricked at her pride more and more.

Had she not proven that she could keep up with the march? That she could be useful and not need—her thoughts spluttered mutinously—not need a nursemaid? Cade was as annoying in his way as Pendarek had been, she grimaced to herself as she thought of the witch Merys' younger brother. That one! He had bullied her and frightened her, yet the thought came to her now how it was he who had known the role that only she could play in that first adventure with the mage Pendravyn.

And, to be fair, she admitted to herself with reluctance, Cade was kind to her for all that he had begun to annoy her. With a rare smile one evening, he remarked that he had only half as much work to do with her assistance. Since Herrell shooed her away with a gruff '*Be off with ye now*' when she would have helped him with their evening supper, Cade led her on forays through the camp.

Everywhere they ventured, careful to stay out of the way of warriors busy with the work of keeping weapons and armor clean and in working order on that long march, Cade stopped to speak a quiet word at one campfire, then another, and was welcomed with a curiously courteous nod and offer of food and drink. He and Cailie would squat by the fire, Cailie listening but not speaking. No one usually spared her more than a glance.

She soon learned that the Shōtar came from over the northern mountains and that the Bulwari came from the reaches of the southern plains. The Dobhuti, foot cavalry whose soldiers ran tirelessly from morn to night, counted nearly as many women as men among their ranks. Cailie admired these women, their hair cropped short to fit beneath their crested helmets. Men and women alike wore short kilted skirts with fitted vests of woven leather.

Tall, supple boots covered their legs above the knees. At night, around their fires, they cleaned the long swords they carried sheathed across their backs and their double, short serrated daggers thrust into a scabbard belted at the waist.

Cailie hung back from shyness when first Cade approached one Dobhuti campfire. Some of the women warriors looked scarcely older than Cailie herself. They nodded to Cade and bade him sit by their fire and drew Cailie forward when she would have seated herself in the shadows behind Cade. Although she could not understand their speech, by their frank gazes and relaxed soft murmurs, she realized that they were questioning Cade about her.

Cade flashed a sudden grin as one young woman smiled at Cailie and spoke rapidly. The others laughed.

"Neave says you must have a gift, Cailie. She swears one of the hounds thought to have her for a meal today before its master called it back."

Cailie smiled in return and dipped her head. It was good to feel welcome and not made to feel that she had no place in this great encampment.

Later, as Cade led the way back to Herrell's campfire, Cailie put a hand on his arm, stalling him.

"Cade, how is it," she paused and met the dark eyes that held her own, his face betraying no impatience as he waited for her to finish. "How is it that everyone knows you?" For one moment she thought she saw wariness and chagrin pass swiftly across Cade's features and she hurried on. "You speak with everyone—no matter where they come from—and they . . . they," she faltered at the look of gentle amusement he gave her and dropped her hand from his arm.

"How could a simple houndsman move amongst great warriors?"

Cailie flushed.

"I didn't mean that—I only meant—" she stammered.

Cade laughed softly, then leaned forward and kissed her quickly on the mouth. His eyes, she had time to note, were the deepest black and sparks stirred in their depths. His lips were soft and warm, and, well, inviting. Her wits confounded, she had no time to protest, or, as an inner voice urged with enthusiasm, to seek a second kiss.

He tucked her arm into his and pulled her on their way.

"Why, sweet Cailie, 'tis only common courtesy to welcome a comrade, no matter how lowly, to the fire."

Cheeks flaming, Cailie yanked her arm free. She still had wits enough about her to realize that he had not answered her question. Every camp they visited had greeted Cade with equal measures, she puzzled it out, of affectionate welcome and respect. Whoever he might be, Cade was more than a simple houndsman's assistant.

Wrapped in his blanket, Cade lay on his side by the fire. The rigid line of Cailie's back told him that she lay awake on the other side of the campfire. Herrell sat like a stone, pipe clenched between his teeth. The embers of the fire were glowing beneath the ashes when at last Cailie relaxed into sleep. Cade bit back a sigh and got to his feet. As always, Herrell nodded and kept his silent vigil at Cailie's side while Cade faded into the shadows.

The gray hound loped away into the darkness, covering miles of mountain trails with an untiring stride. He slowed and left the track at one point to climb to a stony ledge covered in scrub growth. Here the hound lay low and crawled into the brushy cover to peer into the valley. Alaric's banner flew from a high, crenellated wall of the keep at the far end of the valley. Torches burned at intervals along that wall, creating shadows that wavered into shapes as guards patrolled the keep's walls.

Few lights burned elsewhere within those parts of the keep visible to the hound, save for a single tower which stood at the rear of the heavily fortified stronghold as if part of the mountain behind it. A muted light shone in the highest window of that tower—a light which did not flicker as the torches sputtered below. A dull red glow was imprinted onto the stones surrounding the window. When the red darkened to the color of old blood, the gray hound backed gingerly from his perch and slunk back down to the track, staying low to the ground until well away from the valley.

Resting at the edge of a stream, the long form of the hound lengthened and stood warily in the shadows. Cade drew a thin braided cord from beneath the neck of his shirt and clasped the polished oaken oval, his fingers tracing the image of the wolf carved there. As he did so, his features subtly shifted and he seemed to grow taller.

"Sister," he called, "I am here."

Merys appeared in his mind's eye, grave and composed.

"Pendarek? What news?"

"Bakshir yet searches for the power within the holy treasures."

"Ah," Merys' indrawn breath was quick. "Then we have time, still, to make sure he does not succeed."

"Pendravyn has recovered?" Hope flared as Pendarek put the question to his sister.

Her features stilled and hope dimmed.

"He is better." The flat statement discouraged further questions. Merys sighed. "The Star Mage will say no more." Her dark eyes, so like her brother's, searched his face and she frowned.

"And young Cailie? She comes with the army?"

"Yes. She comes."

Merys bit her lip.

"I wish I could see farther." Angrily, she shook her head, the auburn curls dancing. "Why draw the child into danger once more? What part must she play?"

"I will guard her well, Sister."

Merys heaved a sigh and a rush of affection warmed her as her gaze softened.

"It must be hard, looking after the child, but I have no qualms about her safety, Pendarek. Or, should I say Cade?" She laughed, with a gentle teasing, and he answered with a grin.

"Better not to show all our hand to Bakshir, should he look too closely."

"Then go now, least of the houndsmen, back to your camp to watch over the little one—little Cailie." Merys withdrew from his mind before Pendarek answered, his features rueful, a finger stroking his lips.

"If you but knew, my sister, Cailie is no one's little girl now. And I will watch over her," he added softly, although there was no one to hear, "until the end of our days."

The Cherdir

The Cherdir halted at Khasil's command. The plains ran down to the great river—the Dracha—far to the south of the Cherdir's homeland. The shaman ordered a sweat lodge to be built on the bluff edge overlooking the river. Even as Cheruk squatted at his mother's fire, he could see the shaman striding from his pavilion to the sweat lodge. Pausing to cast a satisfied glance at the preparations and then a second, sweeping glance across the encampment, Khasil handed his robes to the guards who stood at each side of the low entrance into the lodge and entered alone, letting the hide covering fall behind him.

The mood in the encampment was subdued; voices were kept low and no boisterous children ran between the tents. The guards stiffened to attention whenever anyone ventured near the clearing where the sweat lodge stood. The slow rumbling of a deep-voiced chanting issued from the sweat lodge. The sound hovered on the edge of consciousness, and Nima was sure that it was this that kept the camp uneasy, for the chant was dark and cold as the winter's ice and her thoughts shrank from the force of it. Khasil needed something—sought some help, some guidance before the Cherdir would move again.

Nima had knelt prostrate like her age-mate on the tent floor until the shaman was escorted to the sweat lodge by two of his guards. Two stood yet at the entrance to the pavilion, a clear warning that no one should approach in Khasil's absence. Glancing at Chella, Nima nodded wordlessly at the two chests by the shaman's chair. Chella rose, took up the sleeping child, and stepped outside the tent entrance. Nima heard the sharp bark of one of the men standing guard, followed by Chella's soft reply to the guards.

"We go nowhere. Just here within your reach, for fresh air and sunlight. Are we not the Cherdir? Do we not welcome the sun and the breeze to our camps?"

Nima suppressed a sigh as Chella did not return. Remembering the cold which seemed to fill the tent when the shaman was at his prayers, she had half-hoped that she would not have to risk the chests. Moving rapidly, her booted feet making no sound on the soft floor of the shaman's tent, she crossed to the two small chests and dropped to her knees before the first. With fumbling fingers, she undid the hasps and opened the lid, throwing a frightened glance behind her at the tent entrance. She caught sight of Chella, swaying in the fresh air with the babe in her arms and spared a small thought of amusement at how the guards' eyes were not likely to look elsewhere when Chella stood before them. Turning her attention back to the chest and its contents, her eyes widened and she bit the back of her hand to keep from crying out. Inside the chest, lying on a black silken cloth, was the great clan-leader's *kerdun*. All the Cherdir knew this by sight, for it passed from father to son at the climax of a four-day celebration when the new clan-chief was installed.

Nima did not touch it, but closed the lid again and latched it securely, thinking furiously. This was not something the high shaman had brought from the ruined city. It

was a thing of power only among the Cherdir—
and most certainly—she knew it instinctively—
the source of Khasil's power over the clan-
chief.

Throwing a nervous glance at the doorway
to the tent, she wiped her sweating palms on
her breeches, took a deep breath, and moved
to the second chest. Whatever purpose took
Khasil to the sweat lodge, she knew that the
ceremonies within would not be hurried. There
was time, still, before he finished. A light,
happy giggle arrested her attention. The child
was awake and clearly delighted to be outside.
Her heart beating hard against her chest, Nima
undid the hasps of the second chest. A thin
red finely woven scarf draped something
within. Taking care not to disturb anything
else in the chest, she pulled the scarf aside
and frowned. A small, clear glass goblet with
an ornate foot and stem lay cradled within the
chest. Twisted gold formed a vine with leaves
that coiled part of the way up the sides of the
goblet and into handles on each side.

With a sense of wonderment, Nima touched
a fingertip to the intricate design, and all but
cried out as she rocked back on her heels in
shock. The touch had sent an arrow of cold
piercing the length of her arm to the elbow.
With shaking hands, she caught her fall, and

reached within to draw the fabric across the goblet again, this time taking care not to touch it. She let the lid down without a sound and did up the hasps.

When Chella's raised voice reached her, she was kneeling upon her bedroll.

"Come, little one, you shall be dry and fed again in just a moment."

Chella's eyes met Nima's as soon as she entered the tent, widening at her age-sister's pale features.

CHAPTER SEVEN

Wolverness Abbey

A flutter of wings woke Cailie's mind from a deep sleep into a lucid dream. She raised a hand as to ward off the wren, then the scent of warm roses assailed her nostrils and her thoughts cleared. The wren! The wren darted at her once more and this time Cailie did not hesitate. Where the wren led, she must follow. Slipping away from her bed at Wolverness Abbey, she did not look back at the pale form lying so still on its cot, nor did she notice the tall sister who lay a hand upon Cailie's white, cold forehead. Kissing the cross she wore at her neck, the sister sent a young novice at a run for the mother superior.

The wren flew on, always ahead of Cailie, who trailed after it with the scent of roses everywhere about her. At last, Cailie became aware of a thunderous sound, of hooves pounding and harness jingling as dust enveloped her. The moment she was aware of the sound, the wren vanished. Afraid now, Cailie whirled about in the cloud of dust, but the wren was nowhere to be seen nor could its song be heard. Had she voice, she might have screamed with the panic which washed through her soul, but the rose scent filled the space about her and steadied her.

Then she heard it, the clear song of the wren. It drew her forward as the wren sang sweetly, and by and by Cailie found herself once more seeing from someone else's eyes. The rider's gaze through which she saw swept the horse-clans, but returned again and again to those who rode at the front of the clans. It came to her as she watched that the rider was working his way forward to some purpose. At last he was positioned in the rear of the retinue of the great clan leader and could clearly see the two young women Cailie had seen before. One of them glanced back and gave a quick, small nod.

"Cheruk," a gruff voice spoke from behind her as a burly horseman nudged his mount past her rider. Cheruk—he had a name now, the young man through whom she viewed this march of the Cherdir, through whose eyes she had watched that scene in the tent, whose bitter sigh had rung in her mind. And, as though some barrier fell when she learned his name, Cailie found Cheruk's thoughts open to her.

Chella, his cousin, urged her horse closer to her age-sister, Nima. The baby turned his face to her, but did not cry and Chella's heart swelled with a sense of pride. He might have been born to the clans, this little one.

Cailie's world swirled about her; she might have spun the spirit of herself into a million shooting molecules if the power of the wren and the rose had not held her to her place. That child! Daniel! But how? How came Daniel to be here with the Cherdir?

'How?' The anguished question echoed in her mind, and she heard Cheruk's angry thoughts buzzing. 'Soon it will be too late. Khasil is driving the clans faster and faster. He must be drawing near to that which he seeks. But, what is it? And how,' again the despairing thought beat at him and at Cailie, though he did not know it, 'how am I to save my sisters and the child?'

And now Cailie knew her purpose, knew why the wren had led her to the Cherdir. Had Daniel been stolen away—for she knew beyond certainty that her brother Trevor and his wife Almeda would never have given up their son willingly—because of his link to her? Because of her forays into the world of wizards and witches as a young girl? But which time? And why now, after all these years? It made no sense, but some part for her lay in this desprate venture, and whatever she had to give, she would. For whoever—or whatever—had brought Daniel to this time and place, she knew there was more at risk than the fate of one small child, however dearly loved.

In the dim chamber, the Mother Superior stood at Sister Condetta's side, her face grave.

"She cannot be roused," Sister Condetta murmured, her brown eyes troubled. "Not by voice or touch."

The Mother Superior nodded, stepped closer to the cot where Cailie's body lay and drew back the blankets covering their patient. Pushing aside one of the hot water bottles, she lay her hand thoughtfully upon the thin shift covering Cailie. Replacing the water bottle and the blankets, the Mother Superior met Sister Condetta's concerned gaze.

"Her body is warm and still she breathes. Do not give up hope, Sister Condetta. Keep the water hot at all times, stoke up the fire to add heat to the room. And pray," she suggested as she withdrew, "pray as hard as you know how."

Pendravyn

"Be you not discouraged, my friend." Looking up, Joss met the warm brown gaze of Merys' eyes. "All is not lost."

Standing up, the witch held a plate to which she added two thick slices of fresh bread to the bounty of roast meat and cheese Hizer-aban had provided for his friends. Topping this with a crescent of sweet melon, she met the puzzled stare of her mate and cocked a smooth brow at him. "We have a guest to feed. Would you care to meet our stowaway?"

With that, she swung about and made for the door. For one stunned moment they sat and stared at her retreating back, and then all in a haste men and boys scrambled from their chairs, Hizer-aban behind them as they raced after Merys.

At the rear of the wagon she stopped.

"Out with you, little vagabond. Your supper awaits you."

A faint rustle and creak could be heard from within, and then a head ringed about with blue-black curls peeked out, disappearing with alacrity at the sight of the party that waited outside.

Merys stepped closer.

"Come, little one. Be not afraid. Show yourself."

After another minute, the dark head bobbed up again and a pair of deep brown eyes looked them over. Another half-minute and a child about the height of Mykael climbed out of the wizard's wagon. Dressed in a *qhahesa* like those the boys still wore, Joss received a shock as the hood fell back from those short, flyaway curls. Their stowaway was a girl! Thin wrists showed as she reached with both hands for the plate of food offered to her.

"My name is Merys," the witch introduced herself, "and these are my friends."

Swallowing a mouthful of bread, the girl replied in a clear voice.

"I am my mother's daughter, Maesa ap-Chan."

"Tell me, Maesa ap-Chan, why have you hidden yourself in this wagon?"

Maesa's brown eyes glinted as she swallowed a bite of melon.

"For this," she said simply, pulling a chain from beneath her *qhahesa*. The quick intake of breath from the knight and his cousin told Joss that they too recognized the image on the amulet which dangled from the chain. Aelfris! Her pale cheeks flushed, Maesa pointed a steady finger at the squire.

"I saw them bring in this prisoner. Sagar—the fat, bald one who plays with evil magic—he told them not to kill this one because having him alive would draw the great wizard Pendravyn into his trap. Sagar planned to take him prisoner, too. Khasil, the High Shaman himself, would deal with the wizard and his friends."

"You know the shaman, little Maesa?" Pendravyn asked curiously. The girl's stony eyes bore into him, unblinking.

"Sagar speaks to Khasil through a black pool of water. I have seen his foul image there."

"And you, little sister," the lady-witch touched her hand gently, "how came you to the household of Sagar?"

Maesa rubbed a quick hand over her face.

"I traveled the roads of the caravanners like the children of Aelfris have always done." Maesa's voice rose in a sing-song fashion and as she spoke, her fingers curled around the amulet she wore about her neck.

"The 'children of Aelfris?'" Pendravyn queried the child in a soft voice, careful not to interrupt her story.

Maesa nodded.

"Yes. For time forgotten, my people have been known by these holy images which we wear, passed from my mother's mother to my mother to me."

"And Sagar?" Merys prompted.

"That one!" Maesa's dark eyes flashed and an angry flush reddened her cheeks. "He chanced upon me in the marketplace and tried to buy my name-sake! The holy image! When I refused him, he tried to steal it from my neck by magic and found that he could not take it without the wearer. So, I found myself a prisoner and have been for nigh unto a month now."

As she directed her dark intent gaze at Joss, a blush crept up his neck.

"There was no way I could escape the compound, and so no one was set to watch me. I was hiding in an empty stall when that one and his companions tried to get away. When the bazorki went for Sagar's throat, I hid myself in this wagon."

The bazorki! Joss' mind wandered from Maesa's words. Where was their four-footed companion? Thinking back, he realized he hadn't seen the bazorki in the courtyard after their arrival at Hizer-aban's. Surely it would not have remained in the wagon without Maesa seeing it. Then, another image caught at his memory—Merys on the wagon seat, and Pendravyn's words came back to him. He and Sir Daven had taken separate paths into the city. Neither had traveled with Merys. Glancing up quickly, Joss saw the lady witch's mouth twitch at one corner as she met his gaze unperturbed. They hadn't been abandoned after all, he thought. Merys had been looking after them in the shape of the gray bazorki!

With an effort, he tore his eyes and thoughts from the witch.

Reaching into the heavy folds of his robes, Pendravyn pulled out the two amulets of Aelfris. Maesa's eyes widened.

"Know you, then, Maesa ap-Chan," the wizard addressed the girl solemnly, "that these amulets may hold the key to an ancient prophecy, and our world may hang in the balance!"

"And Daniel!" Nickolas piped up firmly.

Maesa touched the images reverently, and then prodded the sharper one.

"This one, by the hand of Aelfris himself, was newly given from the heart of Aelfris. And its wearer is dead, else it would never have come into an outsider's hands," the young girl finished, her voice full of grief for its owner.

"If we return you to your people," Merys asked the girl, "will you reveal to us the source of the amulets? For even as you have seen, Sagar serves the shaman Khasil and it is he who seeks to fulfill that ancient, evil prophecy."

Maesa looked long and hard at the amulets swinging in Pendravyn's grip, then squared her thin shoulders and tightened her fingers about the amulet she wore.

"If you will take me home," she told them, "I will plead your cause with my lady-mother, Haesa ap'Chan."

"Well said, little sister," Merys lightly squeezed the girl's shoulder. "That is all for which we could hope. Come, let us confer with Hizer-aban about replenishing our provisions." With a protective hand on her shoulder, the witch guided Maesa through the courtyard, Hizer-aban at her elbow.

"Hmm . . . ." Sir Daven caught Pendravyn's eye. "The caravanners," he repeated thoughtfully.

"It fits," Pendravyn answered, and then took pity on the boys' confused faces. "Sir Daven and I made our way here to Hizer-aban. Living as he does in the heart of Vertain-Sola, Hizer-aban gathers a great deal of information from the traders who supply the city with their wares."

Slowly the rest of the company followed in the wake of Merys and Maesa, making their way inside to a cool, open room, its windows shuttered against the setting sun. Ceiling fans stirred up a lazy breeze. As they seated themselves on cushions, a servant brought fresh, cold glasses of tart lemonade. Pendravyn drank thirstily, and then waved a hand at the merchant as he rejoined his guests.

"Hizer-aban reports that the horse-clans of the Cherdir have left their homelands. They follow Khasil, who seems to have some hold over the Cherdir clan-chief. The caravan routes lie in the opposite direction. We cannot be in two places at once, unless," he paused significantly and stared around the circle of familiar faces, "unless we split up our party."

Squire Persiflas opened his mouth, closed it again without speaking, and then shrugged. Pendravyn's fierce blue eyes seemed remote and cold.

"He has Daniel, the child, and the Alabine Goblet, which he brought out of the ruins of Ka'ma-atl. This much we have learned. Now he marches south and we must seek the rest of the holy treasures before he succeeds in finding them. We have an excellent chance of discovering the source of the amulets, which may very well provide the 'Barque of Justice.' If we split up, perhaps we can rescue Daniel and prevent Khasil from reaching his goal."

"I want to follow Khasil," the words came tumbling from Joss' lips even as Mykael and Nickolas nodded in fervent agreement.

"Hear me, my brave young friends," Pendravyn held up a hand. "Khasil is guided by strong powers, ones I do not wish you to face. Think you on this—if we follow him and fail to stop him, then we are left with naught. Yet, if you will seek the amulets, perhaps they will lead you to knowledge of the ship of Aelfris. Then, we shall have snatched that much from the hands of the Cherdir shaman."

"With the blessing of Aelfris, we will be in a better position to win back your baby-cousin," Merys spoke with quiet emphasis at Pendravyn's side. Maesa sat without speaking on a cushion at the witch's feet, restlessly twisting her fingers together.

"Will you not have need of Monsterslayer, oh Wizard," Sir Daven asked, "to keep you safe?"

"Nay," the old man's face relaxed its stern expression and he winked at the squire. "Methinks you would do better to travel with this stalwart company. Between your trusty sword and the fair hand of Merys, you can do naught but succeed in your quest.

"One harmless old tump-trader will travel faster and with less notice than one riding a warhorse with a great knight."

"Harmless!" Sir Daven choked back a dry laugh of disbelief. The wizard jerked a quick gaze back to the boys and sobered.

"Well, my friends? Will your faith trust in me to follow Khasil and retrieve young Daniel?"

Traveling out of Ithan-Almara with that same magical, ground-eating pace they had experienced before, the boys and their party came to the mighty Dracha River and followed its course south toward the town of Ap'cha. As they traveled they passed the stone rings of abandoned caravanners' fires set along the black banks of the Dracha, or battened down by some wizened willows that grew at the very edge of the great grassy plains they traversed.

Often as many as twenty or thirty such rings made up a single encampment. The manner in which the fire hearths were grouped told much about the caravanners' identity, for as Maesa explained, a caravanner clan led by a single, powerful matriarch would have many small hearths clustering about a larger one. A circle of similar-sized stone-lined fire pits, however, meant the caravanners were tied together by several related females of the same age-group, along with their husbands and children. In one such group as this she clapped her hands with glee and pounced on a stalk of sweetgrass which lay broken on a river cobble.

"See here, Joss-Elder Brother," Maesa named the youth, "this very spot was home for a space to my lady-mother!"

"How can you be so certain?" Joss asked, looking about with curiosity. A hearth was a hearth! How could the girl be so certain as to who had made these? Maesa's dark eyes glistened and she twirled about, counting.

"Five, six, seven hearths! Seven sisters guide my clan, and Haesa ap'Chan is the eldest." She laughed with delight, the first laugh she'd loosed in all their travels, and reached a hand to pull at a clump of grass. "Come, little-brothers," she called to Mykael and Nickolas. "I will show you how to weave these grasses into a fine bracelet for your mothers."

Merys decided they would rest the horses and have a hot meal before continuing, for, as she noted dryly, Ap'cha was not renowned for its cuisine. Making use of one of the fire-rings left by the caravanners, they soon had a fire going. Merys rummaged among the supplies provided by Hizer-aban to prepare a pot of soup to simmer. The smell wafted across their camp.

Helping the squire brush down Rex, who rolled his eyes as contented as Hesperius when scratched between the ears, Joss remarked.

"I've explained and explained what a 'cousin' means, but I don't think Maesa understands."

Squire Daven shrugged.

"She's from a different people, with different customs, Master Joss."

"That's true." Merys reached past the squire to feed a handful of grain to the warhorse. "With Maesa's people, all children of sisters are considered like brothers and sisters to one another. The only difference that matters is age. To her, Mykael and Nickolas and you, Joss, are all brothers, elder and younger."

"Ho!" Sir Persiflas came striding back from a high point of cliff that jutted out over the Dracha twenty yards along the bank.

"Ap'cha's fires can be seen. We draw nigh unto our goal, fair Merys."

The witch nodded, and then bent her head to one side, listening, her body tense, as if some sound unheard by the rest of the camp had reached her.

"Sir Knight," she shouted, whirling about, her robes flying as a stiff wind bent the grass low before her.

Lilly's eyes showed white with terror and Imelda reared, screaming with fear as a dusty, dun-colored figure rose up in a heap before her. Wrapped about with matted, tangled grass from head to toe, it shambled forward with outstretched arms and grasping hands. Gaping holes marked its face where eyes and nostrils and a mouth should have been. Frozen, Joss watched in horror as another, and then another, and then a horde of figures sprang to life around them. Sir Persiflas thrust Monsterslayer forward and a ragged arm was lopped off before it could touch Nickolas, who ducked under Hesperius. Joss' muscles loosened and he yelled.

"Into the wagon, Nickolas!" Grabbing Maesa by the hand, he picked up a river cobble and hurled it at a shambling figure dodging the vicious snap of Hesperius' teeth. Behind Joss, Rex snorted, his hooves shredding another creature. Boosting Maesa onto the wagon into the waiting arms of Squire Daven, Joss saw Mykael send a bucket rolling under the feet of another figure, tripping it. But more of the creatures crowded between his cousin and the safety of the wagon. Scrambling over his brother and Maesa, Joss eluded the squire's grasping fingers.

"Stay inside," he hissed to Nickolas. "Help the squire keep Maesa safe. She's the only one who can help us find Aelfris' ship, the *Hælvedda!*"

Jumping down, Joss grabbed at one of the mares' reins, pulling it taut like a tripwire in the path of two marauding, eyeless figures.

"Joss!" Merys' voice rose above the fray. She held the two mares; they twisted and kicked, slashing out with their hooves at any creature that ventured within reach. "Fire!"

Mykael leapt quickly for a branch and thrust it deep into the cooking fire. It caught in seconds, and he shoved the flaming limb at a creature. Sparks flared and in moments Joss brandished a second torch at his cousin's back. Wherever a spark licked at those grass-covered shadows, the flames swept like wildfire until in seconds only a charred mass of ashes was left.

Thrust, look wildly for the next attacker, thrust again. The nightmare seemed to go on forever, and then the two boys reached the circle cleared about the witch and the long arm of Sir Persiflas and Monsterslayer.

"Fire the grass," Merys directed. As the cousins obeyed, a circle of flame ran around them, encircling the wagon. Merys handed the mares' leads to Mykael, and then raised her hands as she chanted in a tongue Joss could not understand. Flames leapt from her fingertips to the grass and back again.

"Fire to fire, eat up the evil!"

With a mighty surge the fire rose, towering like a wall above them. Then, within a moment, the fire dropped, and with it the wind which had whipped through the grass. No more of those shambling eyeless creatures came forth to attack the camp.

Merys took a cautious step forward and with disgust pushed with the toe of her shoe at one shapeless bundle on the ground. It fell to pieces until only shreds of grass lay before her.

Nickolas and Maesa climbed down from the wagon behind Squire Daven and joined their companions. The squire took Monsterslayer as the knight slipped off his helm.

"What were those things, Merys?" Mykael asked, his voice hoarse with exhaustion.

"Grass-mummies!" came the swift answer.

"See here," her toe indicated the shreds of charred grass. "Nothing within, not even bone. Someone has called to those ancient, sleeping spirits of the dead, those who died in battle on the banks of the mighty Dracha centuries ago! Warrior-spirits roused from their ageless slumber and given form with the only material at hand—the grasses of these plains." Merys' voice was cold, her brown eyes bleak. "That these valiant souls should have been so defiled!"

"Aye," the knight heaved a deep sigh. "But who, my lady-witch, who wrought this evil against us when Pendravyn even now chases Khasil far to the south?"

The witch surveyed the horizon as if some fearsome spirit would make itself known to her, then her chin swept up and she addressed her companions.

"Magic reaches beyond one's fingertips, Sir Knight. I think this bit of evil-doing was sent from afar to stop us in our quest."

"Then we must press on," Maesa declared, and all else nodded agreement. Joss found himself clutching the dragon-pin he wore on his collar with nervous fingers and wished, not for the first time, that Otaghi-Ray were there to help them.

Warily, with Sir Persiflas ahead on the warhorse, Merys led her party into the dispirited town of Ap'cha. A dirtier, colorless place one could not have conjured with a spell, Joss thought as he eyed the surly-looking town. No more grass-mummies came to plague them, although it seemed as if even the dead stirred restlessly in the ground as the witch's party passed. A small square lay in the center of the town, three sides holding long, low warehouses where open bays spilled bales and barrels of good onto the wayfare. The third side held a customs house, where berobed officials measured sacks of grain and other goods, weighing them on huge, over-sized scales. A large alehouse and inn filled the rest of the space next to the customs house. People crowded the square, clustered about the customs' officials, standing in knots before the open doors of the warehouses, and streaming into and out of the alehouse, tankards in hand both coming and going.

"Ho'cha!" Maesa called, jumping up on the wagon seat and stretching her arms high as she waved to a giant of a man, bearded and muscled. As big as the plow horse on his grandfather's farm, Joss observed, as he studied the milling crowds in the central square.

"Maesa little-daughter!" the man cried and lifted her from the wagon seat with a mighty hug. "Your lady-mother was nigh unto singing the first of the death-chants for you! What has befallen you? And who are these good folk?"

Maesa twisted in Ho'cha's massive arms.

"Sing not the death-chants for me, Elder Father, for this company snatched me from the shores of that dark sea. Where bides my mother now?"

"Camped beyond the Eastern Portal with your other mothers, little one. Let us make haste to show them your sweet face!"

Haesa ap'Chan was a small dark woman with eyes as dark and flashing as her daughter's. Dressed in breeches tucked into high soft boots, she wore a roughly woven red *qhahesa* over a shirt the color of honey. Thoughtfully, she fingered the amulet that hung from her own slender neck, one arm firmly around Maesa.

"You have recovered my child for me," she said at last when Merys had told her tale. "I cannot do less than help you retrieve this other lost babe.

"But, know this: the *Hælvedda* is but legend to my people, as to yours. The holy images which we wear—these have come from the dead to the living, borne from the hills and washed in the streams and rivers of the lands we travel. If you will follow, we will show you what we can."

Sir Persiflas cleared his throat.

"Our thanks be with you Haesa ap'Chan, lady-mother and elder sister. We will follow wherever you shall lead."

A bit flowery perhaps, as was the knight's wont, but well before the morning was much advanced, they found themselves turning their backs on the soot-begrimed sod houses of Ap'cha and its dusty, downtrodden square, where the liveliest groups were always those heading out one of the town's four gates, out into the world, away from Ap'cha.

Mykael, riding behind Maesa on Hesperius, commented on the vast, treeless plains that stretched before him with no sign of villages or towns or farms, for as the squire had noted, the earth held its ghosts tightly. So thick and tough were the grasses that no plows could churn the sod and the winds so fierce, with no forests or hills to break their passage, that no one lived permanently out on the plains. These lands were home to birds and small prowling cats which fed on the hares and rodents that burrowed beneath the grass, but no grazing animals lived here—leaving the plains uninhabited on both sides of the Dracha.

"Why do your people, the Caravanners, travel this way, Maesa-sister?" Mykael asked as he and the young girl rode Hesperius next to Pendravyn's wagon. "What do you find to bring back to market?"

And why, Joss wondered to himself, were there so few young boys or elderly men who traveled with Maesa's people?

Maesa pulled at the thick, sky-blue *qhahesa* that she wore.

"Do not your own *qhahesas* keep you wonderfully warm?" She tossed the question back at Joss' cousin without waiting for an answer. "We bring the wool that is woven into these and many other fine goods. Our menfolk tend the flocks of each clan in the winter pastures snug in the Harven Hill-lands to the east."

"And this?" Mykael touched the small leather bag that swung from her side. Maesa's words carried back to Joss as she urged Hesperius to a trot.

"We make those, too. Leatherworking keeps idle fingers busy through the long winter snows."

Riding, riding, riding into the east until at last there appeared like a mirage on the edge of those wiry grass plains the faintest of shadows between land and sky. Foothills! The caravanners' winter strongholds! The witch's company traveled long, hard hours each day, pushing on as if the cold, sharp tongue of winter were already licking at their heels. Joss pushed all thought of Daniel away, praying that Pendravyn would find him safe and sound. Now, he focused all his efforts to helping the journey go as smoothly as possible, helping to keep the thoughts of his brother and cousin from dwelling on the fate of their baby cousin.

The hills, smoky-gray and heather purple, rounded and low, drew nearer and nearer as they followed a well-worn trail. The foothills graced the banks of the River Stürma, and behind them, like smudged shadows, rose the first ranks of the Sturm Mountains. It was Merys, walking the perimeter of the well-lit caravanner camp with its seven campfires—eight with their own drawn into the circle, who found the first sheep, stiffened in a narrow gully.

Haesa ap'Chan squatted beside the dead animal, but did not touch it.

"Dead two days or more," she announced swiftly, "and odd, my lady witch, that no carrion eaters have come to prey upon such a fat prize!"

The sheep was round and fat, although it stank to high-heaven now and its black tongue rolled from its mouth. Beside him Nickolas gagged and Joss put an arm about his brother, turned him away from the gruesome sight, and led him back to camp. Nickolas didn't look well at all, and his older brother worried about whether he was getting sick, as hard as they all pushed themselves each day. Sometimes at night now, Nickolas woke him thrashing about on his blankets. Mykael, who always had a question or a story to tell, often fell silent, staring inward as if he saw something dark in his thoughts that he could not share. Hurry! Hurry! Hurry! That thought drove them all—witch and knight and squire, too.

The next morning they had gone forward less than a mile when Ho'cha swung down from his dappled stallion and climbed onto a patch of rocky ground. Pulling back a scraggly bush, he revealed another stiffened sheep, this one a young ewe. The caravanners muttered amongst themselves, Haesa and her sisters at the center of the group. Then Haesa Elder-Mother broke away and strode over to the turquoise and yellow wagon.

"These are strange omens, Lady Merys," and indeed, the caravanner leader's tight eyes and worried frown were echoed by her sisters and the menfolk who rode with them. "Think you, my lady, that your company can leave your wagon in the care of my clansfolk and ride forth mounted into the Harven Homeland with myself and my scouts?

"For the flocks should all be with the menfolk in the higher pastures. And if these are here, then what harm has come to our flocks?" And the thought 'and to our menfolk,' unspoken, hung in the air between the caravanner elder and the witch's company.

Sir Daven patted Monsterslayer's brilliant scabbard as Rex snorted.

"Lead on, Haesa ap'Chan! We will follow on my warhorse!"

Rex, catching his master's tone, pranced sideways; his black coat shone beneath the morning sky. Merys touched the squire's arm.

"With you, Squire Persiflas, I leave our three young charges. I know your attention to duty and your wits will keep them safe." She brushed Nickolas' cheek with a finger in a light caress, included Joss and Mykael in her reassuring glance. "Follow with the caravanners while we see what wicked mischief has touched the far strongholds of these good people!"

Sir Daven reached an arm to the witch and swung her lightly up behind him on the warhorse. With a quick wave, the knight set their mount after Haesa, two of her sisters, and a caravanner brother.

Squire Persiflas picked up Lilly's and Imelda's reins.

"Come along, m'ladies! Let us make haste."

As the wagon moved forward, a small dark head popped up on the seat. Maesa grinned at Joss.

"My lady-mother said I might ride with you."

Making room for her beside him, Joss scrunched closer to Nickolas and dropped his arm around his little brother's thin shoulders. Nickolas' mouth drooped and his shoulders sagged. He looked like he had lost his best friend.

When the horses could go no further, they stopped late in the evening to make camp. The night seemed cold and dreary in spite of the campfires and not even their evening meal seemed to warm them. Nickolas pushed his plate away, his food barely touched.

"I think I'll go to sleep now, Joss," he told his brother, forestalling the protest on Joss' lips. "I'm tired."

"I'll be along soon, Nickolas." Maybe, Joss cast a worried glance at his brother's back, if Nickolas turned in early, he'd get the sleep he needed. Joss followed him to the wagon and fussed with his brother's blankets, tucking them close about Nickolas. He sat on the wagon seat listening as the young boy settled to sleep before he made his way back to the campfire. No stories were being told that night. A mournful *fila*-horn player blew a sad little tune on his flute-like instrument. The notes curled skyward with the silver spiral of smoke, and Joss shivered.

Mykael stirred and yawned.

"I think I'll turn in, too, Joss."

"Me, too!" Maesa stretched. Joss stepped around the fire and touched the squire on the shoulder.

"Good night, Squire Persiflas. Wake us when you need us in the morning."

The squire nodded and resumed his silent contemplation of the fire.

The Cherdir

Nima went down on one knee at the water wagon, turned the tap, and watched as water trickled into one of her buckets. The slightest of pressures on her ankle told her what she wanted to know—her brother Cheruk was beneath the wagon.

"*He,*" she would not say the shaman's name, "has the clan-chief's *kerdun.*" Her voice was pitched low and carried no farther than the wagon before her. Cheruk made no sound, but his fingers tightened abruptly on his sister's booted foot. "The other chest," she added and shivered involuntarily at the thought of what lay there, "holds a small goblet wrapped in gold vines and flowers. I have never seen its like, Cheruk.

"*He* must have brought it with him from the ruined city of Za'Matl. And," her voice dropped even lower and Cheruk, straining to hear, felt the shudder that ran through her, "when I laid a finger to it, all the cold of a thousand winters threatened to engulf me where I knelt."

Switching buckets, she dropped to one knee again as the second bucket filled. Cheruk's voice issued so quietly from the darkness that the sense of his words settled within Nima's mind almost unspoken.

"If we can retrieve our father's *kerdun*, my sister, we can end the shaman's power over the Cherdir. If you or Nima are alone again, try to steal it from him. Leave the other for now. With our father restored, the horse-clans will be more than a match for Khasil."

Nima stooped to pick up her buckets. She handed one with a shrug to the guard who appeared at her elbow without a glance or word and strode ahead of him to the high shaman's tent.

CHAPTER EIGHT

Young Cailie

Cailie's eyes were closed, feigning sleep, but her ears picked up the soft footsteps as Cade left their campfire. She heard his footsteps as he returned hours later. Where had he gone? Away from the camp, she was certain. But where? And why?

A sharp wind found its way down the neck of her jacket the next morning as the army marched higher and higher into the mountains. Cailie rode as always behind Cade. She knew where they rode and why now, but still she could see no part for her to play in the battle to come. Her pewter talisman—the wren—warmed her pocket, but she had seen no sign, nor heard any word spoken about the wizard Pendravyn or the witch Merys. Except for the witch's brother Pendarek, she knew no other mages or witches, and there was no one whom she could ask about why she should have been drawn into this conflict. Clearly, magic had taken her from the safety of her home—but she was only a simple child of Caristoke. She could hardly approach the great lords who marched so grimly into battle and ask them if they knew of Pendravyn or the witch Merys.

The troops halted late in the afternoon, and Cailie slid from their mount before Cade could help her. She felt rather than saw the quizzical glance he sent her, but did not look at him as she waited for the hounds. But the hounds did not come coursing through the camp to them and the camp itself was unusually quiet.

Cade put a hand on her arm and Cailie jumped. His dark eyes were grave and met Cailie's for a long moment. 'How deep they were, those eyes,' Cailie thought inconsequentially, as though if she looked long enough, the whole of the universe would be reflected in those twin pools. She shook her head to clear her thoughts as Cade removed his hand and pointed in the direction of the hillside above them.

"Come with me, Cailie."

They climbed up the hillside to a small ledge of granite thrusting out over the road below.

"There," he pointed again, and Cailie's throat tightened as she looked out over the high mountain valley spread out below them. At the near edge of that valley, tucked against the mountains from which they had come, rose a black keep. At the heart of it stood a tower that seemed carved from the mountains behind it. Even in the light of day, Cailie could make out the dull red flush that seemed to burn the very stones of the tower. Without volition, her hand clutched the pewter wren that lay within her pocket and its faint warmth reassured her.

She swung about to face Cade and a shock went through her. His gaze was remote and cold, as though he looked through her at something she could not see. He passed a hand over his eyes, gave a small sigh and took her arm again, leading her back to camp. But not before she glimpsed the worry and the pain that he masked almost before she saw.

The army flowed into the valley before the black keep and spread out before it, but stayed well out of reach of the keep's walls and its defenders. From her position at the rear of the troops, Cailie shivered.

"Why aren't Alaric's forces attacking?"

She realized she had spoken her thought aloud when Cade answered.

"Because his position is secure. The king's nephew has men and supplies enough to withstand our siege. And Bakshir the Drummer strives even now to unleash dark forces to aid them in their quest for dominion."

Cailie's throat was dry and she licked her lips and swallowed before she could speak.

"What do you mean?" But she knew already and shivered again. Once before she had been drawn to battle with an army arrayed before a keep. Then, she had been within the besieged keep, and the witch's brother, Pendarek, had led her on a desperate gamble to aid the king's forces, sending her alone against dark magic to play her part in winning the battle that raged far above the bowels of the keep.

"Alaric and Bakshir seek power that is too dark to be contained by human forces. They are testing each piece of the treasure for power. It is only a matter of time before they hit upon the piece they seek. We shall soon know if they have succeeded, for we shall be no match for what will be unleashed upon the world."

Appalled, Cailie stumbled to a halt, rounding on her companion with a ferocity that erupted from her.

"Then why are we here? Why," her arm swept the forces arrayed on the valley floor before them, "if there is no hope of success, why have so many come to die?"

Cade's gaze followed her own, so bleak and resigned that Cailie nearly wept with despair.

"We must hold Alaric's attention because there is yet one hope, sweet Cailie, that all is not lost."

Shocked beyond comprehension, Cailie did not note that endearment, not then, not until later—much later would she remember. She sputtered and could not find her voice for a moment.

"We—we're just a diversion? All of these warriors?"

"Yes." Cade strode forward. He stopped when Cailie did not follow, her eyes wary.

"How," her whispered voice was rough and she cleared her throat. "How do you know all of this, Cade?"

"Everyone knows this," he answered, the words catching in his throat. He cleared his throat and continued. "They came knowing this. If Alaric and Bakshir succeed in finding that which they seek among the holy treasures of Rebehan, then an evil will be loosed that will rend this world in two and we shall all perish."

He had known this—her eyes lifted to the forces gathered to fight—the Shōtar and the Dobhuti, they had all come, knowing the odds, but willing to die. She thought of her family— safe in Caristoke and innocently ignorant of the battle about to be waged to save the world as they knew it. A rush of fierce determination filled her—she would do whatever was asked of her—until her final breath, she would fight to stop Alaric from succeeding, and failing that, yes, to delay him for as long as possible. Without another word, she followed Cade back to camp.

Herrell looked around anxiously as they returned.

Cade took Cailie by the shoulders.

"Keep close to Herrell, no matter what happens, Cailie. He's an old warrior with plenty of experience and the heart of a lion."

"But," bewildered, Cailie gripped Cade's jacket. "Where will you be?"

A brief smile flashed and was gone in an instant.

"Here, until I am needed elsewhere."

His grip slackened, but still Cailie held tightly to him.

"Wait, Cade. What was it you meant—that there is yet hope? Who comes?"

His head jerked suddenly, as if in answer to a call. He pulled himself free of Cailie's grasp and squeezed her hands hard.

"It begins. I must go, Cailie."

And he was gone, disappearing into the milling camp-helpers as Cailie stood, her heart thudding hollowly in her chest and her eyes burning with tears she refused to shed. The high scream of a horse reached her along with the terrible baying of the hounds. The battle for the keep had begun. She lifted a beseeching gaze to Herrell.

"What do you want me to do? Where am I needed?"

Herrell kept Cailie busy helping tend to the wounded. Adept not only with his cooking herbs, the old warrior ministered with poultices and ointments for wounds and herbed drinks for pain, his touch sure and gentle with those who made their way unaided to him or were brought forth on makeshift litters. There were not as many of these as Cailie had feared—not yet. The besieged had not sallied forth from the keep to engage any of the forces arrayed before them in open battle, but arrows found their mark among those too foolhardy or green to stay well out of range of the keep's archers. Great siege engines were being assembled and made ready to attack the walls and gates. Burning masses of pitch and slag were catapulted over the keep's walls, but still the keep's gates remained closed.

The Cherdir

Emira listened to Cheruk's terse report, stirring at the mention of the clan-chief's *kerdun.* Her soft voice, when she spoke, did not carry beyond the small cook-fire before her tent.

"I think you must be right, Cheruk. The *kerdun* holds the key to Khasil's power over your father. But the other—" she shook her head. "Tell your sisters to leave the goblet. We know nothing of its power and it seems as though only harm will come to one who would dare take it."

"But what if," Cheruk forced his worst fear into the open, "what if we cannot defeat Khasil as long as he has that ancient goblet of power? I say we try to take it and put it beyond his reach!"

His mother's dark eyes were thoughtful.

"And if, in taking it, you put others at danger? Or cause it to fall into worse hands?" She bit her lip, thinking. She tapped Cheruk's hand gently and shook her head. "Without the warriors of the horse-clans behind him, I think even this thing of power is not enough to give Khasil that which he seeks—else, he would not have led us from our homelands."

Cheruk closed his eyes in thought a moment, before jerking his head once in assent. His mother was wise, but it felt all wrong to leave that ancient goblet in the high shaman's power if they could take it from him.

'Cold. The cold of a thousand winters. . . .' Despair filled Cailie's mind as Emira's words conjured a memory—clear and sharp—from her youth. The Cherdir shaman had taken the Alabine goblet from the ruined city. She herself had laid that same goblet within the basin at the foot of the stone carving in Ka'ma-atl. The carving which had spoken to her and enveloped her in the cold of ancient stone. What had its final warning been? That if ever the goblet were taken from Ka'ma-atl, the cold would consume her. As it threatened even now, despite the efforts of all the good sisters of Wolverness Abbey.

The Caravanners

Tossing and turning in the cramped confines of the wagon, Joss woke, came wide awake, and looked about at the sleeping forms of his companions. Rather than risk waking Nickolas with his sleeplessness, he gathered up his blanket to go sit by the fire. As he crawled towards the rear of the wagon, his cousin lifted his head.

"Joss," whispered Mykael, "why are we moving? It's still dark!"

Stunned, Joss realized that he hadn't been tossing, the wizard's wagon was rolling forward, jolting along the rough trail.

Scrambling from their cocoon of blankets, the two boys stepped over the sleeping figures of Maesa and Nickolas to make their way to the front of the wagon. Cautiously, ever so cautiously, they cracked the door and peered out. A dark bulky figure, silhouetted against the faint starlight, clucked the reins. But who? The head moved slightly as if the person had heard the door easing open. Squire Persiflas hesitated a moment, listening, before turning his head forward once more. Joss shivered and smothered a gasp. He could feel Mykael trembling at his side. The squire's eyes glowed red as hot coals, not a sign of humanity within.

Carefully, slowly, so slowly every nerve in his body cried out with the need to scream, Joss closed the half-door to the front of the wagon and crawled behind Mykael to Nickolas and Maesa. With hands over their mouths, the boys woke them. Nickolas came instantly awake, his eyes alert. Jerking his head to the back of the wagon, Joss gathered up his blanket and motioned for the others to do the same. Mykael stuffed bread into the pocket of his *qhahesa* and slung a flask of water about his neck. Reaching the rear of the wagon and peering out into the darkness, Joss was met by the gaze of Hesperius, who, quite unlike his usual cantankerous self, remained quiet and cooperative as the boy clumsily undid his lead rope. When the mule was free, Joss beckoned to his brother, cousin, and Maesa. Mykael climbed out first and steadied Nickolas as he swung over the edge. Maesa went next and Joss followed, shoving Pendravyn's cooking knife into his waistband right before he climbed out.

Leading a docile, uncomplaining Hesperius, the quartet headed away from the trail into the foothills. As soon as they were out of sight of the mountain trail, Joss boosted Nickolas and Maesa onto the mule as Mykael explained what had happened.

"Ought we to go back down the trail to the camp?" Maesa questioned, looking longingly back at the trail. With a pang, Joss remembered that she had just been reunited with her mother and her clan.

"He might come back," Nickolas pointed out, shivering, "once he sees we're missing." Josh gulped and thought quickly. Where could they find help and reach safety?

"Maesa, can you guide us to your winter encampment?"

Outlined against the night sky, her small figure shrugged.

"I think, yes. But let us move away from the trail as fast as we can and find a hole to hide. We'll need light enough to travel safely and swiftly."

Her suggestion made good sense. Mykael and Joss led the mule and his lightweight burden into the night. Stumbling along, a worried thought nibbled at Joss like the bubbling edge of panic. What had happened to the squire? At every hoot of owl or snapped twig, he jumped and felt Mykael do likewise. Hesperius never faltered, however, and they trudged onward into the night. Then Maesa stirred, slipping her blanket back from her head as Nickolas' strained whisper came through the darkness.

"Up ahead, Joss! There's a bunch of big rocks. Maybe we can hide somewhere in there!"

As they cleared their way around a thicket of dry, heady pines, the tumble of boulders loomed before them. Urging the mule up the slope, Joss winced as a pebble rolled from his path. The night seemed to be full of ears, listening for the slightest hint of their whereabouts.

"Joss, look!" Mykael stopped dead in the process of pulling aside a weedy branch from a scraggly shrub that grew in the hill face behind the boulders. A blur of darkness, deeper even than the gloom of night, loomed before the boys.

"A shelter!" Maesa whispered hopefully.

Swinging down from Hesperius' back, she fumbled in her leather bag and a moment later held a glowing squared metal stick aloft.

"Do you think it's safe here, Joss?" Nickolas' hand tugged at his brother's shirt.

Stooping, Joss picked up a handful of loose pebbles, flinging them as far into that dark space as he could. The pebbles rattled and rolled and pinged as they struck the floor and other rocks, but no other sound came from within.

"Come on," Joss urged, and together they stepped forward into the rockshelter. With some relief, Joss saw that it was dry and large enough to shelter both the children and Hesperius, who allowed himself to be led inside without a fuss. The boulders hid the shelter from below and when Mykael had pulled the branches back into place, they were invisible to anyone on the slope below them. Hesperius settled comfortably along the rear wall of the shelter. Deep enough to keep out the wind, the rockshelter also kept out the chill, and for that Joss was grateful.

"Here, Nickolas." He settled his brother's blanket more securely about the younger boy, noting as he did so that Nickolas was shivering. Stooping, he used his cupped hands to scoop out a hollow in the sandy floor with the aid of Maesa's light. "Snuggle in beside Hesperius," he urged his brother. As Nickolas lay down and curled up under his blanket, Joss held the light in turn as Maesa and Mykael followed suit, scooping out hollows for themselves. Only when the other three were settled did he hand the light back and make himself a makeshift bed between his companions and the open shelter edge. Hesperius gave a plaintive snort. Mykael reached over his cousin to give the mule's side an affectionate pat. No need to stand guard; Hesperius would let them know soon enough if anyone—or anything—approached their bolt-hole.

"Try to sleep," Joss whispered, keeping his voice as low and even as he could, "we're safe now." Safe . . . an odd choice of words, he reflected sleepily, given that they were four children alone in the wilderness with only a mule and a kitchen knife for protection, but tiredly he realized that fear had left him, and with that knowledge, he slept.

The soft patter of rain woke him. Maesa was gone, Joss noticed with alarm, but as he rolled to his knees, she ducked inside the cave mouth.

"There's a sheltered place, behind the bushes, to go outside if you need," she told him matter-of-factly.

As Joss came back, making quick work of his need, Mykael sat up and rubbed his eyes. Maesa reported her observations.

"The rain has washed away any tracks we may have made last night."

"Good. Let's have some breakfast. Everyone take some bread, and we'll share the water."

"There's a spring at the side of the cave where we can water Hesperius and refill our flask before we leave," Maesa added.

"Why don't we wait a little while to see if the rain lets up," Nickolas suggested with a glance at the gray skies visible through their screen of bushes, and Maesa nodded, her dark eyes solemn.

That feeling of safety, probably a false sense of security, Joss admitted to himself, still held this morning, so he didn't argue that they should leave right away, but accepted his chunk of bread and fed Hesperius his share. And still it rained. An hour later the rain was heavier than when they had awakened.

Walking Hesperius up and down the length of the shelter, Mykael kept up a running patter to the squire's mule. The ornery old creature had a soft spot in his heart for the boy and would go for him when no one else could budge the stubborn animal. Maesa, stick in hand, was drawing a map for Nickolas in the sandy floor of the shelter, showing him the trails they would need to take to reach the winter stronghold of the ap'Chan clan. Nickolas, his blond head bent close to her dark one, interrupted now and then to ask a question.

Arms crossed against his chest, Joss stared at the rain, a sense of urgency riding him. What had caused the squire to head out into the night with them in tow, away from the Caravanners? And those glowing red eyes—he shuddered. Well, there was no help for it. They would just have to hope that they reached shelter before the temperature dropped—or before they ran into something—or someone— they would rather not see. Still the rain drummed steadily on the rocky ledge beyond their shelter. Joss cast his eyes about them. They had certainly found themselves a snug hideaway. The walls arched smoothly, cuplike over their heads, and the sandy floor provided a cushioned place to sit or sleep.

Eyes narrowed in thought, Joss stood up and walked over to the back wall. That smooth wall seemed almost too smooth, and now, up close, he ran his hand across the surface. It felt as slick as glass, not a rough spot anywhere as his fingers slid across the cold, fine-grained stone of that wall. Turning slowly, he surveyed the shelter. The sandy floor. The sand could have been weathered from the rock face of the cliff, eventually creating the sand deposit, but would it have weathered the cavity so smoothly and regularly? But, if nature was not responsible, then what? Or who?

Frowning, Joss pushed idly at the sand at the edge of the back wall with his foot. Here the sand was shallower, for an inch or so of the bare rock floor was uncovered. And a dark scar or seam appeared where his foot had scraped the sand back from the wall. Flinging himself to his knees, he scooped urgently at the sand.

"Hey, Joss!" Mykael flopped down on his knees beside his cousin as Nickolas and Maesa peered over his shoulders. "What are you doing?"

The sand flowed away from that seam and as Joss worked, the seam was revealed as a squarish form. Mykael joined him in scooping away the sand and suddenly they both stopped. Nickolas' elbows fluttered with his rising excitement, like a songbird about to take wing.

"It's a trapdoor, Joss! There's a secret passage under our hidey hole!"

Beneath the boys' hands an iron ring fixed in the center of a square of the rock floor lay partially revealed. In seconds they cleared away the rest of the sand. Then together the two pulled on that ring and found, to their great surprise, that the stone lifted out as lightly as a woven grass mat. A dark cylindrical shaft sank deep into the ground, but as Maesa held her light forth once again, they could see handholds cut into the rock, descending into the tunnel. Out of that darkness, equally surprising, flowed a cool, sweet breath of air. Joss met the gazes of his brother and Mykael and, over her light, Maesa. The light broke and glinted from the image of Aelfris that swung from her neck.

"Well?" he demanded.

"Let's do it," Mykael responded. Maesa nodded abruptly, and Nickolas grinned. Hesperius munched on a bush growing in a cleft of the floor at the edge of the shelter, his contented gaze resting on the children. Who knew what terrible things might wait for them underground, Joss had time to wonder. Or where the tunnel might lead, or who might be waiting at the far end or at this end when or if, he gulped, they climbed back out? But, all his doubts faded as that sweet breeze strengthened, drawing him like a promise to the secret entrance.

"I'll take the light, Maesa, and go first. You and Nickolas come down next when I give the all clear, followed by Mykael last."

They nodded.

"Oh boy, oh boy!" Nickolas' enthusiastic whisper reached his brother and Joss could have sworn the young boy's feet would have lifted from the ground if Mykael hadn't urged him away from the edge of the trapdoor. Maesa handed Joss her lightstick, and he stuck the cool, glowing metal in his pocket as he carefully felt for the first step down with a cautious foot. Looking up once, three pairs of dark eyes danced in the reflection of the light. Another dozen steps and his reaching foot landed on solid rock. Whirling about, he held the light high and saw a tunnel opening before him into the heart of the hillside.

"All right," Joss called softly, although who else he thought might hear, he didn't ask himself. Above him, Maesa descended those rough-hewn steps as Joss held her light aloft. Next, Nickolas' boot-shod feet appeared, and then as his friend stood beside Joss, Mykael climbed down in Nickolas' wake.

Together the four walked into the darkness, the cool air flowing about them. Almost it seemed as if a breath of salt air rushed in from some ancient inland sea. Deeper and deeper they trekked beneath the hillside. As Joss' hand brushed the smooth wall of the tunnel, he was startled to feel a vibration, then a low humming echoed all around them. Mykael, trailing his hand along the wall on the other side of the tunnel, paused.

"Like putting your ear to a seashell."

He was right, the low sound boomed and echoed hollowly like waves rolling into shore and out again. Where did this tunnel lead? Still that sound echoed in the tunnel, but softly, as if at a great distance in space, or time. Their pace increased. Fairly racing now, the four companions rushed on towards the source of that sound, that salt air.

Now words, snatches of songs, voices resounded, called, spoke to them. As if caught in a dream, they ran on and on. At last, panting, they burst into an open space. Silence rushed around them, a deafening silence as they gasped for breath. Maesa's small stick of light was dwarfed by the immense cavern in which they stood, gaping at the huge, shrouded ship which sailed into eternity in the heart of a hillside in the Harven Hill-lands. Their feeble light reflected from the gleaming polished wood of the ship, caught, ran like wildfire up the rigging, flaring the great, taut sails to light. And as they stumbled forward, awed, drawn by the powerful, majestic beauty of that ship, Maesa gasped and clutched her image.

"Holy Mother!" The words were squeezed from her trembling lips. "The *Hælvedda*, mother-ship of truth!"

Here, before their eyes, the very ship they sought! Buried beneath a hill and as much use to boy or wizard as Hesperius would have been trying to climb down that tunnel! Nickolas stirred; he must have been thinking much the same thought for his shoulders drooped. Touching his brother's arm, he squared his shoulders and squinted up at the *Hælvedda*.

"There must be something here, Joss. Something. Or why else would the ship be mentioned in that old prophecy?"

His brother shrugged, blew out his breath in frustration.

"Come on, we're wasting our time. We've got to find the knight and Merys. This can't help us. We'd never be able to move it!"

Even as Joss spoke, Mykael's head lifted sharply as though he heard a sound the rest could not. Nodding once to himself, he darted to the side of the ship and clambered up its rigging as fast as Minou the cat up a tree before any of his companions could move. When Joss would have run after him, Maesa stopped him.

"Wait, Joss-elder brother! We'll board her together or not at all."

Joss nodded once, jerked his head at the ship, and ran for the rigging draped over its side. He paused to boost the girl and Nickolas up onto the ropes before he started climbing on their heels. Pulling himself over the railing, he saw Nickolas and Maesa shivering, waiting for him, frozen to the deck. For in the very center of that narrow, cleared deck a statue sat facing them. The face of Aelfris, as cold and stiff as marble, stared at them. Carved on an immense throne, his hands resting easily upon its arms, he was garbed in a long robe that swept the deck. A shining, heavy medallion, dwarfing the one Maesa wore, glinted on his chest.

Bearded, his features seemed set in a gaze that looked right into one's heart, seeing all of one's whole life turned inside out, weighing the good thoughts and deeds and happiness against all the sins of lies and greed and meanness of spirit. Before that serene, unmoving gaze Joss felt as though eternity itself stood to judge him, and he held his breath, afraid to move. With one hand, he reached out to pull Nickolas closer, protectively to him as Maesa held his other hand.

Then, his heart pounding, he saw and understood. The awesome figure that commanded the *Hælvedda* was no simple carved stone statue, but Joss swore later, the very spirit of the great king, Aelfris himself. On the deck of his ship, the king watched over his people from death as he had done a thousand or more years ago, when life was his. A shadow moved and Nickolas squeezed his brother's hand until it hurt. Mykael stepped from the shadows surrounding the statue.

Slowly, raptly, the boys' cousin approached that entombed king. Joss tried to cry out, but no sound came forth from his throat. His feet might have been chained to the deck. Aelfris' hands appeared to loosen their grip on the throne. In a horrifying, slow-motion fashion, time distorted space and the dead king's eyes focused on Mykael, his lips moving. Their cousin's small, thin shadow climbed even higher upon the throne. Those great calm hands rose, blurred; the mouth opened again. No whisper of sound or sense reached the three by the ship's rail. Mykael disappeared from sight behind the flowing sleeves of Aelfris' robe. For one terrifying moment Joss thought he was gone forever, and then the arms relaxed to rest upon the throne. The king's gaze blazed beyond the pale blond blur of Mykael's head and probed like a beam of light—cold and strong and relentless—into their very souls.

The next moment, a statue sat before them once more. Mykael backed down from his position on the throne one careful step at a time, his eyes never leaving the grave face of the dead king. At last his feet touched the decking. Raising one fist in a respectful salute, he turned, and seeing his cousins and Maesa, walked to where they stood and without a word climbed back down the rigging. Equally silent, they followed him off the ship, then up the tunnel in a journey that seemed much shorter, up the shaft into the rockshelter where Hesperius still munched on his bush and rolled his blue eye at them in mild curiosity as they emerged from the passage's mouth.

Without discussion, as Joss climbed out last, he and Mykael let down the trapdoor and watched with numbed amazement as even its seams disappeared, the ring melting away until only rough, bare rock remained. Nickolas and Maesa scooped sand over the floor. Together they evened the sand out as best they could, before trooping outside where the sun now shone. Digging out the last of their bread, Joss passed it around and Nickolas did the same with the water flask. As they ate, the chill that had engulfed them in the cavern lightened and was gone. Mykael, sighing, looked around at his companions and began his story.

"His spirit spoke to me, there in the cavern." Mykael's dark eyes widened as he remembered. "Aelfris the Just bade me come and stand before him. And so I did. His eyes opened and it was like being bathed in light, Joss! He said that the *Hælvedda* had found our hearts pure, that we should have that which we sought. And that the *Hælvedda* would stand against evil on the 'River-That-Is-No-More.' Then he . . . he gave us his blessing and it was time to leave him in peace."

CHAPTER NINE

Young Cailie

By nightfall, weary to the bone, Cailie sank down beside Herrell at their campfire. Fear bit at her. Where was Cade?

"Rest, Cailie," Herrell commanded with a gentle tap upon her hand and draped a blanket about her shoulders. Despite her worry, Cailie fell asleep as soon as she lay down, rolled in her blanket. Tossing about from side to side, she dreamed that she was marching endlessly among a thousand faceless warriors, dread filling her with each step until her whole body shook.

Her body *was* shaking, Cailie realized as she woke with a start in darkness to find Herrell half-kneeling beside her.

"Quickly, Cailie!" He pulled at her arm to yank her to her feet. "Alaric has sent part of his forces from behind to destroy the army's supplies. Hurry!"

Herrell half-dragged her along as he ran. Wide awake now, Cailie could hear yells and curses as people fled the supply camp, and, more frighteningly, the sound of steel on steel as those who could drew weapons to defend themselves and slow the assault. Here and there among those who fled, some carried torches, so that Cailie caught a glimpse of faces looking as grim as she felt. People were crowding together now, caught between the attackers behind them and some of their own fighters—warned by those who first fled—who were rushing to defend the army's flank. In the melee, Cailie caught sight of a dark head and whipped about sharply, stumbling, her arm torn from Herrell's grip as the crowd surged around them.

"Cade!" She struggled through the heaving mass of panicked people and called again. "Cade!"

Once more she thought she saw a dark head and pushed on. Where was he and why hadn't he found his way back to camp? Cailie pushed her way clear at last and found herself in a small grove of trees. She caught her breath and scanned the grove about her, for the sudden silence among the trees seemed ominous, unnerving her. From the safety of the grove, she could see flames where wagons had been fired and the sprawling, fierce fighting that raged across the rear of the encampment.

The battle at the rear moved closer even as she hesitated, and Cailie saw that she was trapped. Retreating further into the woods, she reached a streambed where bushes grew on both sides and screened the water. She followed the stream and ran, the sounds of battle echoing about her, propelling her on until at last she could run no further. Taking a deep breath, she crossed the stream and pushed through the bushes on the other side. Here the land rose and, hidden for the moment, she collapsed, panting against a fall of boulders at the foot of the hillside. Once more, the clang of swords and jingling of armor warned her and she scrambled up the boulders, up the hillside, coming down on her knees again and again on the uneven footing. At last she was up as high as she could get; the trees below her rang with shouts and the hard clash of steel against steel. Cailie backed up until rough stone bit into her knees; she had stumbled against a low overhang. Low enough, she decided, that she could crawl beneath the rock and remain unseen, yet still see down the hillside when the darkness lifted. Please let the keep's forces be driven back, she prayed, but the sounds of fighting came so near and loud that she was afraid to even think.

At last it seemed to her that the ringing of metal against metal dimmed, and Cailie sank into a kind of stupor in her rough hiding place. Until there was light enough to show her that the way down was safe, she was stuck under the low overhang. She dozed fitfully, her cheek pressed against the rock beneath her, the wren digging into her chest.

When she opened her eyes, a faint shift in the darkness heralded the coming of daybreak. She lay indecisive, cold and hungry in the cramped space beneath the overhang. Should she slip back down the stream to the grove below before full light and try to make her way to the army's encampment? Then she froze as a scrabbling noise reached her. Someone moved out there on the slope below her. Cailie sucked in her breath and strained to hear. Oh where, she wondered wildly, was the witch Merys and Pendravyn? If she had been pulled into this distant war because she had some part to play, now would be an excellent moment for them to rescue her.

She gulped as another scraping noise reached her. Even Pendarek, the witch's brother, would be a godsend. 'Where are you when I need you, Pendarek?' she whispered. She could see his eyes as clearly as if his face were before her. Those eyes! She had spent days looking into eyes just like those . . . Cade's eyes. And Cade, the realization struck her, had been welcome in every camp—not Cade, the houndsman's assistant—but

Pendarek, the witch's brother. Her cheeks flamed. He had kissed her! But why hide his identity from her? Another slithering of loose rock warned her that whoever climbed so stealthily was nearly upon her. She closed her eyes tightly, childishly hoping that if she could not see, she would not be visible to anyone else.

Then a scrabbling noise and a whine reached her, and before she could react, a moist nose poked itself into her hair and a rough tongue rasped her cheek. As Cailie opened her eyes, the hound whined again and crawled under the overhang with her, forcing her to retreat farther back into the confined space, then farther and farther until she realized that the ledge marked a narrow fissure that opened into the hillside behind her. She pushed at the hound. She wanted out—back into the light and fresh air. Then she noticed that the hound had gone still and tense in every muscle, as quiet as the rock around them, making no sound.

A sharp grunt came close by and she froze, one hand convulsively gripping the hound's fur. Beyond the dog, she could see legs outlined against the opening of the overhang.

"Higher, up there, we'll be hidden in the rocks until nightfall, then we can make our way back into the keep." Another hoarse grunt and she watched in silent horror as the legs disappeared. The muted thud of heavy boots penetrated her panic as the men climbed up the slope above the overhang where she cowered. She was trapped in this narrow space.

Panic bit at Cailie and only the presence of the hound, blocking her way, kept her from taking her chances and bolting from her shallow cave. Those voices had spoken of making their way back into the keep—Alaric's men. Enemy, then, and positioned directly above her. She rested her head against the body of the hound as a waft of cool air soothed her fevered thoughts. The hound lifted its head towards her, whined softly and licked her cheek again.

Cailie eyed the hound thoughtfully, then licked her finger and held it up. A small, cold current of air dried the dampness on her fingertip. Air—moving towards her, out of the depths of this fissure. The hound whined again. What have we got to lose, Cailie thought wildly, and shifted her weight so that she could free her left arm from beneath her and sweep it into the space behind her. No barrier as far as she could feel. She slithered as quietly as possible farther back into the fissure of rock and the hound crept after her. Still there came no wall of rock to block their passage, and rolling on her side to rest for a moment, she put her hand up to feel the space opening above her. The fissure was opening out the farther they traveled back into the hillside.

Before long, it had widened into a tunnel high enough that Cailie could walk stooped over with the hound at her side. Along with the steady current of fresh air came a pale, flickering light and soon she heard the telltale sound of water dripping somewhere ahead of them. The hound stopped, his tail thumping her leg. Cailie crouched down and put her arm around the dog's neck, stroking him while she considered their plight. She would go forward and discover the source of the water. If it was sweet, they could drink their fill, and she would wait until cover of darkness before retracing her steps to the opening of the overhang on the hillside.

The Caravanners

Nickolas was the first to break the silence which followed Mykael's tale.

"But how, Mykael? How is Aelfris' ship going to sail on any river?"

"Yes, little-brother," Maesa chimed in sadly, "you saw the great ship yourself there in the heart of the mountain!"

Nodding his head glumly in agreement, Joss shrugged his shoulders without speaking.

Grinning, Mykael reached into his shirt and slowly, reverently, pulled from around his neck a chain of heavy gold links. Nickolas gaped and Maesa clutched her amulet. Hanging from around his cousin's neck was the great seal of Aelfris himself, the *Hælvedda* etched into a relief so true to life one could almost feel the seas parting beneath her hull.

"Oh my!" Nickolas, up on his knees, leaned over to touch a finger to the gleaming medallion. "We'd better find Merys as soon as we can!"

Maesa looked up, judging the sun's position in the sky, then stood up and dusted her hands. She pointed to the far hills.

"If we go that way, we'll come out onto a winter pasture. There will be a trail leading down to one of the encampments. We can reach Haesa-mother then, and through her, your friends."

"Come on, you," Mykael coaxed the mule away from his bush. "We've got places to go and people to find!"

Yes, the uneasy thought crossed Joss' mind, if the squire didn't find them first. Where was Squire Persiflas? And what had caused their faithful friend to steal away with them in the middle of the night? He saw in his mind's eye those gleaming red eyes and a shudder ran through him.

With Nickolas and Maesa astride Hesperius once more, *qhahesas* pulled close against the stiffening wind at their backs, the group headed farther into the Harven Hill-lands. Stopping only to rest briefly and let their sturdy mule drink, they pushed on until the sun slanted long shadows across the slopes and trails they followed. The wind now keened at their backs, stirring a sense of dread within Joss. He knew only too well that the very air around them could become a danger—a cloud, a mist, even the grass itself could rise up to attack them on this desperate quest. On the thought, a flutter of wings pounding the air flashed before him. Mykael ducked and halted in amazement as a tiny helidar hawk settled on the arch of Hesperius' neck. The old mule snorted once, but made no move to rid himself of this wild passenger.

Bright yellow eyes widened as the hawk's gaze met and held Joss' own.

"I think it won't be far now, Maesa little-sister, before we reach your mother's clan."

Warily, the girl's bright eyes shifted from the boy to the hawk, while Nickolas sat without moving a muscle and peered over Maesa's shoulder at their visitor.

With a dip of its head in Joss' direction, the helidar spread its golden-tipped wings and launched itself into the air. Circling once, it headed north along the trail and within moments had disappeared from sight. They were safe, Joss guessed, or would be as soon as Merys found her way back to where Haesa ap'Chan and her band awaited the witch's return.

They came into the clearing where the clan camped as the day was drawing to a close. A scrim of rose and tangerine clouds lay across the sun, the air in this sheltered valley washed fresh by the morning's rain. Haesa ap'Chan advanced with her sisters, flanked on one side by Merys and the squire. Sir Persiflas strode forward a pace before them. Pendravyn's yellow and turquoise wagon was drawn into the circle of wagons about the campfires.

"Maesa little-daughter," cried one of her mothers, "what do you mean by running off into the night?"

Maesa waved a hand at her mother and slid from Hesperius' broad back, leaving Nickolas still astride the mule.

"You will not believe what has happened," Maesa called out, running towards her mothers. As she ran the sun dropped from beneath the clouds as full and fiery as a deep coal blazing beneath the ashes of a fire. Long red fingers of light stretched out as if to protest the fading of day. One such ray fell directly upon the advancing knight. His eyes, glowing, reflected red, mad, inhuman.

"Maesa!" Joss yelled, too late as she ran past Sir Persiflas, who flung out his arm about her neck and clasped her to him.

In the stunned silence which followed, Maesa's ragged breathing could be heard across the clearing, and then the knight spoke.

"Give it to me," he demanded harshly, "or this child shall suffer for your refusal!" Maesa whimpered once as his arm tightened. Haesa ap'Chan's involuntary step forward was halted by the slim arm of Merys barring her way.

Mykael's dark eyes were full of fright and his face paled, but he never wavered.

"No, you shall not have it!" was all the answer he made.

The mailed arm of the knight closed even tighter against Maesa's fragile neck.

Then a sound split the tension and the fear rampant in the clearing—a sharp, high, imperious trill of notes, demanding and ordering that evil should depart! In a wink the red gleam was gone from Sir Persiflas' eyes, and his arm dropped. As a badly-shaken Maesa fled to her mother's arms, the knight sank slowly to his knees, eyes closed, head bowed. The squire and Merys and Mykael hurried to him. Joss cast a quick, worried glance up at Nickolas, and then stared in astonishment.

His brown eyes soberly eying the knight, Nickolas put the tiny silver piccolo to his lips once again and loosed a gentle lullaby of a melody as the sun dropped at last below the horizon.

Merys and Squire Daven carefully eased the helm from Sir Persiflas, who stirred and yawned mightily, then curled on his side sound asleep like a babe. The witch's bleak gaze met Joss' above the knight.

"Hied away on a wild goose chase, my young friends—lured away to leave you at the mercy of evil. What befell you? What accursed spirit took over this good knight?"

Shaking his head, Joss told her in halting words of their flight, the shelter they had found, and their discovery of the tunnel that led into the heart of the hill. Reverently, Mykael drew out the great amulet of Aelfris, causing a shocked murmur to arise from Haesa ap'Chan and her clanfolk. Then Merys drew Nickolas close for a brief, hard hug, and the squire shook his hand gravely.

"You have freed the knight of the evil spirit that hid within him. We are in your debt, young master!"

"Look, you!" Joss dropped to his knees beside the sleeping knight. A thin black cord was just visible about Sir Persiflas' neck.

"Wait!" Merys stayed Joss when he would have pulled the cord free. The witch turned to the squire. "Has the good knight ever worn such a cord about his neck?"

The squire shook his head. "Never!"

Merys knelt and pulled the cord free, her hand wrapped in a corner of her cloak. At the center of the cord a small leather pouch was tied. Pulling her amethyst crystal free of her cloak, the witch passed it over the pouch, again without touching it. Her eyes met those of her companions as she gingerly lifted the cord free of the knight's neck, although she avoided touching the bag.

"A finding spell and a binding spell and a memory charm. This amulet bag must have been laid about the poor man's neck when he was taken captive in Vertain-Sola. He did not remember it or notice it hanging there, it bound him to those allies who seek to help Khasil fulfill the prophecy, and it sent him off seeking the *Hælvedda*." She dropped the cord with its bag on the ground some distance from the members of the camp and pointed her crystal at it. A thin, concentrated beam of purple light shot into the heart of the amulet and instantly a flame blazed. Within seconds, the bag and its contents were consumed.

"Come now," Merys encouraged the boys and the squire softly, "let us join the ap'Chan for their meal. We have much to do this night, and your help may be needful."

The squire's hand closed comfortingly, warm and secure, about Joss' own. From the corner of his eye he could just make out the blanket-covered form of the knight. Nickolas, Mykael, and Maesa slept in the wizard's wagon that night, guarded without by Ho'cha, whose massive shadow paced the length of the wagon, along with several other elder-fathers and brothers, all sinewy and lean and as fierce-looking as the high mountains of the Harven Hill-lands.

Joss' attention was drawn back to the fire, round which sat Haesa, her sisters, and their clansmen, and opposite them Squire Daven and himself, the lady witch Merys, who took from her robes a rough rose quartz ball. This she placed in the center of the fire. Together, the assembled company regarded that ball of stone as the flames leapt and crackled over its surface. As the fire caressed it, a glow appeared within the ball, spreading slowly to the surface, and as it did so, the rose quartz cleared. Within the heart of that ball, a movement could be seen. A small form grew larger, then larger. Someone gasped as the form resolved into the head of a man with a trim white beard and mustache. White hair escaped from a squashed black turban, and small round spectacles slid down his long nose. Pendravyn! His piercing blue eyes seemed to bore directly into Joss', then he nodded once and his image was gone as if it had never been. The rose quartz, veined and reddened by the fire, became only a rough stone ball again.

As Joss moved his stiffened fingers in the squire's grasp, a sudden gust of wind blew up from out of nowhere, fanning the little fire into a quick, leaping blaze that scattered sparks among them. Breaking rank as they scooted away from that shower, Joss heard a cough behind him echoed by a startled exclamation from Ho'cha.

"Darned nuisance, those sparks!"

Swinging about, Joss' eyes widened and a foolish grin escaped him as he took in the sight of Pendravyn, absently brushing a cinder from his beard. His shrewd eyes, behind the glasses, took in the sleeping knight, the guarded wagon. Merys slipped an arm about his waist and hugged him to her with a small murmur of relief.

"I feared for you, my love," she told him. With one arm he embraced her in a gesture of reassurance that spoke more clearly than words. His other arm drew Joss into that circle of warmth.

"Ho, Squire Daven," the wizard greeted his friend. "Would you bring me drink? Let me but wet my parched throat, and I would hear your tale of woe."

Merys told him then of the attack by the grass-mummies, their journey into the Harven Hill-lands, and the possession of Sir Persiflas.

"I wondered, my dear," Merys finished, her brow furrowed in thought, "who it was that followed us, harried our efforts? I could find no sign of them though I sought them."

Pendravyn, striding back and forth before the fire, halted and stroked his beard.

"Khasil." Heavily he dropped the name of the high shaman like a stone into the quiet circle of firelight.

"But," Squire Daven objected, "you were chasing him leagues to the south of us!"

"Aye, truly, he moves ever south," Pendravyn answered tiredly, sitting at last by the fire. "But I could not come nigh unto his camp, such are the safeguards he has set about him."

The squire raised a brow at the old wizard.

"Khasil draws strength from an ancient force—one that feeds him power not of his own. How this is so, I could not discover. 'Tis a power that draws evil like bees to a flower full of nectar. The shaman has allies ever willing to aid his quest."

"But," Joss began, shivered, and said no more.

"Oh yes," Pendravyn replied to the boy's unspoken question, "I might have broken through his wards about the Cherdir camp, but I feared for the child if I did so."

"Before I could learn more, I heard you calling and so I came." All at once the wizard looked old, far older than his twinkling eyes might suggest.

"He has the goblet and the child, and we have—."

"We have the *Hælvedda*, the '*Barque of Justice*'."

Unnoticed until he spoke, Mykael approached Pendravyn and pulled the heavy, golden image from beneath his *qhahesa*.

For a long, long moment no one spoke as the firelight played over the carved surface of the amulet, sending light chasing shadows like waves spraying the slender hull of Aelfris' noble ship.

Pendravyn grasped the youngster by the shoulders.

"Chosen by Aelfris himself to bear her," the wizard murmured, and then his gruff voice cleared. "You are a stalwart young warrior, Master Mykael, to stand before the king himself and bear his shield into battle! Well done!"

Mykael's shoulders stiffened as though he recalled that moment when the dead king's spirit had placed the golden amulet about his neck. Proudly he touched it, and then slipped it beneath his outer garment again.

"And," Pendravyn's eyes sought Merys' across the dying flames, "we have also this much. Whilst I followed the Cherdir south, one night I begged a night's shelter in a small village. The houses were built on stilts above a shallow lake. Herat the Net-maker and his wife

S'lia gave me shelter." The wizard's voice grew soft and singsong as he told his story.

"The people of the lake are brown and smiling, dark-haired and soft-spoken. Such was Herat and his brothers and his sons and daughters. But S'lia, his life-mate, she had hair the color of a bright copper kettle, wild with curls, and eyes as green as deep, still pools of water. Her skin was fair and brushed with freckles from the sun.

"It seems she was raised by a pair of *dhasan* merchants on the coast. *Dhasan* is a strong fiber, twisted into ropes or slender threads for nets," he explained to the company gathered about the fire. "The *dhasan* plant grows only along the southern coast in marshy lowlands flooded by the warm current of water that brushes onto land from the Western Ocean at this one place in all the world.

"Herat, like his father before him, traded twice a year with his *patani* or lifelong trading partner from the coast. This S'lon, his trading partner, it seems, had a beautiful young cousin who met Herat on one such trading trip and on the next she came back with him as his life-mate."

"And?" Merys prompted.

"And," Pendravyn repeated, "S'lia told me a story about her birthplace—the walled seaport of Escran with its ruined House of Avat'ar!"

"What?!" A collective gasp met this unexpected news.

"Aye," Pendravyn drank off his cup of ale before going on with his tale. "Generations before, the nobles of the House of Avat'ar lived in a castle above the port of Escran. Twin children were born to every generation—always the firstborn. And always given into their hands—whether they were two sons or two daughters or a girl-child and boy-child—were the Crossed Swords of Avat'ar.

"But the proud and noble line was cursed and for the first time in memory, one of the twins was stillborn. Then the family fell prey to deceit and treachery. One by one the family members died off until the House of Avat'ar was no more."

The dying embers of the fire reflected the wizard's sad tale. Pendravyn took up a stick and poked at the embers. Firelight gleamed in his glasses as he straightened.

"So," he smiled crookedly, "we have a direction in which to go. The town of Escran still flourishes on the coast below those ruins. By the stars, we may learn aught of the Crossed Swords!"

"Escran," Squire Daven mused, scratching his chin, "that lies beyond the marshes on the coast, does it not?"

"Aye," Merys answered. "And on the other side of the marshes stretches no-man's land, the Fenmarsh of Otaghi-Ray." She cast an amused glance at Joss and the two shared a secret, knowing smile.

Otaghi-Ray! Unconsciously, his hand felt for the dragon pinned to the collar of his shirt. The great, solitary ruler of the Fenmarsh, the magnificent pink dragon! Otaghi-Ray had bestirred himself from his marshy stronghold to save Joss' life once upon a time—Joss' and the witch's! A special bond had been forged between them. But this time, there was no call to venture into the Fenmarsh, for their need drew them to Escran and the ancient, walled town where the House of Avat'ar lay in ruins on a hillside. Would it yield up its secrets? Would they find it before Khasil? Would they, Joss gulped quickly, be in time to rescue Daniel?

"Hold onto your faith, little-son." Haesa ap'Chan's dark eyes met the boy's curiously. "Your strength will serve you well."

His strength? Joss looked at his young body and shook his head doubtfully, never thinking of the other kinds of strength one might find deep within oneself.

The Cherdir

Khasil's white braids swung about his face as he paced back and forth before his customary seat in the tent, his meal untouched. Chella exchanged a despairing glance with Nima, who held the baby in her lap. Khasil seemed determined to spend the night pacing; there would come no chance to steal the clan-chief's *kerdun*. The high shaman seemed nervous, for he kept flicking short glances at the child, who sat murmuring and cooing, his hands waving as he grabbed at the tips of Nima's braids, which were wrapped in bright red and blue leather thongs.

At length the shaman came to stand before them, though he did not speak. Chella kept her eyes downcast as Khasil stood there murmuring under his breath. The child paid him no attention, but continued his game with Nima's braids. Abruptly, the high shaman snapped his fingers in front of the babe's face. The baby in Nima's lap lifted his head and gurgled in a high-pitched tone at Khasil. The shaman's face burned and he uttered a sharp rebuke or command, Chella could not be certain which, because once again the high shaman used a tongue she did not know. But it made no difference to the child, he swung his fat fists before him and gurgled louder. Khasil slapped his hands loudly together. Taken aback, the child started, and then stiffened, his body straining to stand against Nima's legs. Now he crowed at the shaman; there was no mistaking the tone of his voluble outburst, chattering, challenging—though he had no words to throw at the shaman. Now it was Khasil who rocked back on his heels, eyes narrowed. Abruptly, he stepped back and whirled about, throwing a last order over his shoulder as he did so.

"Quiet the brat before I am forced to do so myself!"

Nima shifted the baby in her arms and soothed him; as she did so, she exchanged a small triumphant smirk with her age-sister. Chella smothered her laughter. Truly, this child had the heart of a Cherdir warrior!

Pendravyn

The morning's hushed notes trilled like a chorus of striped warblers, and on top of this sounded the high, sweet call of Nickolas' piccolo. The young boy sat cross-legged on the wagon seat and repeated his call, his serious brown eyes lightening as Squire Persiflas sat up, stretched like a cat, and beamed at Nickolas.

"Good day to you, Master Nickolas! Would you help me see to Rex the Warhorse and Hesperius? See how the one stamps his mighty foot and the other—! Hesperius! Eat not your blanket, you most impatient and bad-tempered creature!"

Giggling, Nickolas jumped from the wagon and rescued the tattered blanket from the mule, who brayed in complaint.

By the time the sun climbed free of the morning chill, the wizard's company took their leave of Haesa ap'Chan and her clan. Maesa hugged Merys and solemnly shook Joss' hand and Nickolas'. Before Mykael she paused, and then they grasped each other's hands.

"From this moment forward you are known to us as Mykael ap'Chan, Aelfris' chosen and our adopted clan-brother! May your journey be blessed, may you return some day to visit us, your other family!"

Mykael ducked his head and looked beyond Maesa to the gathered ap'Chan clanfolk.

"Let me bring honor to my ap'Chan clan! I will strive to do my best and if Aelfris wills, someday I'll come home to the Harven Hill-lands again!"

Then Maesa dropped his hands, and Sir Daven clasped his arm and drew the lad before him onto the black war charger Rex. Joss and Nickolas clambered into the wagon. Pendravyn, on the seat next to Merys, clucked to the white mares, and the turquoise and yellow wagon rolled west out of the Harven Hill-lands. Squire Persiflas trotted alongside on the mule.

CHAPTER TEN

Young Cailie

It was clear as the tunnel progressed through the hillside that Cailie and her four-footed companion were traveling in the general direction of Alaric's keep. No matter, then, where it might lead, she would have to turn back to reach the army and safety. Cailie's jaw clenched and her hand tightened in the hound's thick coat at the thought of moving ever closer to Bakshir and Alaric's stronghold. Sighing, she released the hound and ventured forward one cautious step after another. Within a few more yards, the tunnel opened up enough so that she could stand upright. It ended in a cavern with a pool centered in its floor. Darting glances about the space, Caile could see no evidence of the presence of others. She ran forward eagerly and dropped to her knees by the pool. The water was clear and cold enough to cause her hand to ache as she brought the first handful to her mouth. She could see through the depths of the water to cascades of bubbles that marked the spot where a spring fed the pool. The hound dropped at her side and thrust his muzzle into the water. Cailie drank deeply, before splashing water on her face and drying herself with her shirttail.

Pale light reflected from the surface of the water and flickered along the walls. Cailie stared, seeking its source. Her throat constricted. Three-quarters of the way around the pool, what she had taken for a stone ledge was a step and beyond it, another, and another. Rough-hewn steps led the way up to another, wider, taller tunnel. It was from this opening that the glimmer of light reached the cavern and its pool of sweet spring-fed water.

This must be, she thought with a sickening thud of her heart against her ribcage, the keep's source of water, and she had blundered straight into the enemy's reach. Her hand clutched at the wren, seeking reassurance. It lay warm within her fingers. Warm? Startled, Cailie pulled the talisman from her pocket. Warm. Then she was safe where she was—at least for the moment. She studied the cavern about her, puzzled. If this place were being used by the keep's inhabitants, where were the torches that should have hung from the tunnel and the walls, to light the way for those who would surely come here regularly to fetch water? The hound nudged her hand and then put his nose to the ground, sniffing. With a glance back at where she stood indecisive, it loped around the pool and up the stone steps.

"No! Wait!" Cailie cried, then thrust her hand across her mouth as if to stifle the sound already escaped from her throat before she chased after the hound.

The shallow stone steps climbed and twisted and still the hound bounded ahead of Cailie. She rounded a bend to stagger against the seated hound. He had stopped on a small landing and Cailie caught her breath in shock. Before them was a wooden door, bolted shut. Her eyes narrowed, and she moved closer. A rusted iron ring was set into the door and an iron bar held it securely closed. From the looks of the rust on the bar, the door had not been opened in long years. But why was the bar on this side of the tunnel? Her fear eased a bit. No one was using this passageway to reach the spring-fed pool below. Puzzled, her gaze swept the landing. To her right, a much narrower set of steps curved upward into darkness around the door. This time the hound took the stairs slowly, matching Cailie's cautious ascent.

Narrow slits set high on the walls of the stairwell let light in, and occasionally, Cailie caught the rumble of voices or a sharply barked command. Each time she halted and held her breath, fearing discovery at any moment. Letting her breath out slowly, she climbed onward until no sounds of bustle or voices reached her. At some point the steps beneath her feet became squared blocks and the rough stone walls were replaced by carefully laid courses of black masonry. She and the hound were climbing their way higher and higher up on the mountain-side of the black tower. The realization came to her as she eyed the difference in the wall, but even as dread filled her, she did not retreat. With one hand guiding her way and one clutching the wren in her fist, her steps never faltered. The layer of dust that cushioned the sound of their passage reassured her that this secret way had not been used for long ages.

The passage ended at a small landing no more than six feet by six feet in width. No doorway opened onto this landing, unlike the earlier landing below. The hound sat at her feet and waited. Waited for what? Cailie wondered. There was light, and Cailie lifted her gaze to the walls above her, searching for its source. Directly before her, two of the narrow slits were illuminated with a flickering light. Like firelight—or torchlight. She moved forward, running her hands lightly over the wall. No door revealed itself, so she explored the section of wall farther to her left. At length her search was rewarded when her fingertips traced the raised edge of a small rectangular panel no bigger than the palm of her hand, set chest high. Exploring further, she discovered that her fingernail could slip between the panel and the wall behind it.

Cailie grasped the panel and pulled, but it did not budge. Pushing at it from the side yielded no better result. The hound watched her intently, but made no move or sound. Trying again, she pushed at the small stone panel from the bottom and was thrown off guard when it slid silently upward, revealing the back of some heavy drapery through which a pattern of light fell across her hand. Leaning forward for a closer look, Cailie found that she could see into a chamber whose walls were covered with intricately designed tapestries. These were worn thin in some areas, like the one before her, she guessed. Torches within the chamber revealed fantastical beasts woven in forested settings, and a door situated at the far end of the room from her vantage point. With no light behind her, she reasoned, wiping sweaty palms upon her breeches, no one within the chamber or entering it, would notice anything untoward.

Craning her neck so that she could see more of the chamber, Cailie caught herself before she cried out. A low divan had been pushed against the chamber wall to her left, making room for a large table. From the chairs along the wall to her right, it was clear the table had once stood there. Now a sumptuous velvet cloth dangled from the tabletop and upon this was heaped a bright jumble of dazzlingly colored and gleaming objects. Within this mass, she could make out the intricate form of a jewel-encrusted cross, strands of gemstones carved into beads as big as a copper tabutz, and small, ornately worked caskets of gold and silver, lids thrown open to reveal necklaces and goblets and rings spilling haphazardly upon the table.

Her mind boggled at the sight of those treasures. No, she amended silently—one treasure. The holy treasure stolen from the monks of Rebehan. Here in this tower room, where Bakshir and Alaric might retrieve piece after piece to try to wrest from them the secret of the treasure's power. What was it Cade had told her? 'They are testing each piece of the treasure for power. It is only a matter of time before they hit upon the piece they seek.' Cailie clutched the wren as if it were her lifeline, her only route of safety away from the black tower. She could retreat, back the way she and the hound had come, and make her way into the ranks of the forces assembled before the keep. To do what? Lead warriors back through that narrow crack unseen? No one in full armor, nor indeed, much bigger than she herself, would be able to traverse that crevice. And what if someone could? What then? Lead them here to stand before a small hole in the wall and peer within at Alaric's stolen treasure?

'*Think, Cailie!*' She admonished herself, pushing past the fatigue and hunger that gnawed at her. Think! The stairwell led only to this room. No passageways branched from it, no other landings existed except the first one they had encountered and that one was barred from inside the tunnel. There must be access, she reasoned, to the hidden stairwell from the chamber before her. Who could guess why it lay hidden here? A way for the tower occupants to reach what was essentially a private pool below. And a spyhole, to return to the tower unseen. But, where was that access gained? How?

Frustrated, Cailie forced herself to examine the wall before her in detail—first above, then below the peephole. When her search came up empty, she tackled the stretch of wall to her right. Systematically examining every inch with her fingers, she swept them as high as she could reach and swept down again to the floor.

She was nearly to the corner when her fingers brushed another edge of stone. It was, she discovered, shaped like the first panel. Wasting no time, she pushed it up and frowned, for no light appeared. Then the touch of a cold nose to her hand made her jump and swallow the scream that threatened to escape her.

The hound swung its gaze away from Cailie to the wall beside her. Cailie staggered back against the wall. A portion of the wall between the two stone panels had disappeared without a sound. A doorway, hidden behind the tapestries, had opened into the chamber from the passageway. Hastily, Cailie regained her position by the peephole and peered anxiously into the treasure chamber. The door at the far end of the room was still closed. Despair filled her as she contemplated the treasure before her. She could not possibly carry the treasure away even if she could take it unseen. The hound nudged her leg and Cailie looked down, meeting its unblinking gaze. No, she could not, even with the hound's help, carry the treasure back to camp.

But, slowly an idea formed from her whirling thoughts. Maybe it wasn't necessary to carry the treasure all the way back to camp. With a sick feeling in her stomach, Cailie moved to the doorway and pushed at the tapestry before her. There! It opened smoothly along a seam centered in front of the hidden doorway. Like a shadow, the hound pushed into the room ahead of her, went directly to the door, and sat on its haunches facing the door.

'*So be it*,' Cailie thought wildly, hysteria bubbling too near the surface of her mind for comfort, 'bark once if foe and twice if friend approaches.'

Working as quickly as she dared, Cailie pulled the corners of cloth together, forming an unwieldy bundle of treasure and sparing not a moment to marvel at the beauty jumbled before her. Her makeshift sack hit the carpeted floor heavily, but its clank was muffled as she lowered the bundle to the floor. The hound stiffened and Cailie's heart pounded until she was afraid its frantic beating could be heard throughout the keep. Dragging the treasure to the doorway concealed behind the tapestry, she pushed the bundle before her onto the secret landing. Quickly she brushed at the carpet pile to remove the traces of her work, and fled behind the tapestry, pausing only a moment to make sure no sign remained of her path to safety. The hound came with a bound and was barely through the gap when the heavy fabric fell back into place. Cailie was grasping the stone panel to her right, pushing it hard into place, when her ears caught the sound of a bolt being thrown. The secret doorway sealed, she had the peephole panel shut before the first shout reached her ears.

Sinking to her knees and shaking, she threw her arms around the hound and buried her face against its side. The treasure was hidden—for how long, she did not know. Coming to a sudden decision, she straightened. She would take something with her—one thing only from the jumbled items of the monk's treasure, to prove that she had taken it, to show Herrell and Cade—anyone who might be able to retrace her steps and spirit the treasure away from Alaric's and Bakshir's reaches. And if, she shuddered, Alaric did find the rest of his stolen treasure here in this secret passageway, maybe that one thing she took would be the thing of power which he so desperately sought. But which piece? Cailie pulled back one corner of the cloth and stared at the mass of gems and tankards and jewelry, crosses and goblets and crowns that made up a fraction of the holy treasure. She knew no better than Bakshir or Alaric which piece to select.

A faint clamor of sound reached her from the chamber behind the wall. Panicked, she reached blindly into the jumbled pile and grabbed a small, ornate goblet. This would do. Small enough to hide if need arose, and yet enough to prove her tale. With all the heavens willing, perhaps it would be enough to stop Alaric and Bakshir.

Pendravyn

Time stood at their backs like a relentless reminder of the race they ran. The wizard's wagon flew out of the Harven Hill-lands, along the River Stürma to the mighty Dracha River, as Lilly and Imelda trotted with that enchantment which ate up the distances they traveled. The Dracha left the Arvaal Plains behind as it flowed south and dropped into a broad flat valley where natural levees kept the river flowing between its banks.

Each morning and each night Nickolas drew out his piccolo and piped a few notes to awaken Sir Persiflas or to send him to sleep. The good man did not remember the evil spirit which had possessed him, and for this the boys were glad and did not tell him. Meanwhile, Mykael and his precious cargo were never far from Pendravyn's side or the sharp bared blade of Monsterslayer carried by the knight.

Farther south the party pushed on, until bone-tired and pinched with worry, the wizard brought them to the sleepy walled port of Escran. The gates to the town lay open to the sun and cheerful groups of merchants and house-mates and boisterous school children streamed into the town or out again. No one paid the slightest attention to the wagon as they entered the town and made their way to a small crooked house at the end of a forked lane. A painted shingle beside its red door proclaimed *Master Lofario—Optometric Specialiste*. An eye doctor? Sir Daven caught Joss' bewildered glance and dropped a slow wink as Pendravyn stepped up to the door and beat a quick greeting with the knocker.

The door flew open. A short man with a trim yellow beard, snapping black eyes, and an embroidered waistcoat showing under a voluminous white robe paused with his mouth open, then barked.

"I trust you will pay in cash this time, old man!"

The squire and Sir Daven guffawed loudly as Master Lofario ignored Pendravyn and held out both hands to Merys.

"M'lady, m'lady, Merys, welcome to my humble abode. Please, come in and let me bring you a cup of tea, or ale," he added with a sideways glance at Pendravyn. Then the little man burst into laughter.

"You are an old rogue, Master Pendravyn! Come, tell me! What is't that you have need of now?"

Seated in the doctor's study, lined with books and masks and a collection of knives, the boys listened as Pendravyn explained their mission.

"Hm-m," Master Lofario tugged at his waistcoat. "The House of Avat'ar lies in ruins, that is true enough. The crumbling stones can be seen from the town square, but I do not think, mind you, that anything could lie hidden in those ruins. Certainly not the great emblems of that once noble house—not the Crossed Swords!"

"Have you ever heard," Sir Persiflas inquired, "what might have become of those swords?"

The doctor shook his head, gazed absently at the tidy top of his desk, muttering to himself as he rummaged through the drawers of his desk. After a few minutes, he selected a paper from a bunch he'd taken from a drawer and pursed his lips, silently reading whatever was written there. Joss let his breath out and heard Mykael and Nickolas do the same as the little man looked up sharply and snapped a finger against the paper.

"A letter from a former patient of mine, S'bry. Prettiest little chit of a girl. Married . . . ."

"Ahem!" Pendravyn prompted his friend, who glared at the wizard.

"Who married," he repeated firmly once more, "a fine fellow from Eltaba, a few leagues southeast of here. Seems S'bry ran into old Nurse Hetta in Eltaba. Woman must be older than the hills now, but she used to be the younger nursemaid in the House of Avat'ar or what remained thereof. After the last of the family died out, she left Escran and went home. To Eltaba," he pointed out with a sniff for Pendravyn. "If anyone alive might know what became of the swords, it's Hetta."

Impatiently, Joss' eyes sought the door.

"Tomorrow, Joss, m'lad." Pendravyn's grave blue eyes seemed fathomless. "We'll be on our way at first light. Lilly and Imelda must rest."

And Pendravyn, too, Joss thought guiltily. Not to mention the lady witch Merys. It was by their magic, after all, that the group traveled as quickly as they did.

"Rest, m'child." Once more the wizard might have read the boy's mind. "We shall all rest tonight."

The road they traveled the next morning on their way to Eltaba skirted the reed-filled shores of Lake Enshan and coiled and twisted back upon itself as it wound through a band of low hills. Sturdy wooden bridges spanned creeks, leading into the level farm fields that surrounded the placid town of Eltaba. Narrow farm lanes ran between the tall, flowering hedges which fenced the fields.

As the wagon approached the crossroads of the main road and one such hidden lane, a tangle of riders spilled out of the lane across its path.

"Hired soldiers!" Sir Persiflas cried and swung Monsterslayer free as the powerful muscles of the black war charger rippled into motion.

Pendravyn's arm swept Nickolas and Mykael into the wagon behind him. The crowd of riders swirled and parted as Squire Daven urged Hesperius forward. Two slight young men, back to back on small mountain stallions, fought off their attackers. As Monsterslayer flashed in the sun, Sir Persiflas smashed his mailed fist into the shoulder of first one mercenary, then across the back of a second, knocking them winded from their rangy mounts. The squire ducked and dodged, Hesperius' wicked yellow teeth snapping on the backside of one stout fellow leaning into the fray. With the odds now in favor of the two young locals, the hired troop fell to pieces, its members scattering in all directions. As Sir Persiflas and Rex gave chase to the last of the mercenaries, the rescued pair slid wearily from their horses. Pendravyn drew up the reins of the mares, and they halted at command, Imelda stepping in place before she settled by Lilly's side.

One of the young men, his fair hair falling across his eyes, held an arm stiffly against his right side. His brother—his twin, Joss saw as they drew closer—supported him with an arm around the waist. Merys stepped down from the wagon as it halted.

"I know the healing arts," she told the pair. "Will you allow me to see to your wound?"

At nods from the both of them, she approached the duo and helped them to a stone block set at the crossroads. The squire took hold of their horses, while Pendravyn handed the reins of the mares to Joss, his blue eyes narrowed as he studied the brothers before him. Slender as young saplings and as tall and straight, two pairs of green eyes flicked from Merys' quick fingers to the wagon, to the squire, to the knight, and back again. High cheekbones marked pale-skinned faces, although the seriousness of their features seemed alien to those faces, as if they were much more used to laughter than such dangers.

At last the witch tucked the ends of her bandage into the taut white cover over the young man's wound. Now both young men seemed to breathe a sigh of relief, and the one whose wound she had tended offered his hand to Merys.

"I am Allyn, the miller's son."

"And I," his twin spoke in a slightly husky voice, "I am Aline." Brushing the cap from her head, the girl loosed a fall of long blonde tresses. She grinned and her hand tightened on her brother's shoulder.

"The miller's daughter, I presume," Merys remarked dryly.

Aline threw back her head and laughed, a happy, delighted sound that echoed across the fields. Her brother grimaced as though any movement, however small, caused him pain.

"We are traveling into Eltaba," Pendravyn told the pair after introducing his companions. "May we offer you our company and protection?"

Two pairs of green eyes quickly conferred, and then two heads nodded.

Joss crawled into the wagon with Mykael and Nickolas as Allyn was helped aboard the wagon seat with Merys and Pendravyn. Aline rode alongside, leading her brother's horse. Sir Persiflas and the squire flanked the party.

"I wonder," Pendravyn stated curiously, "at rogues and brigands attacking so close to Eltaba."

Again Joss was aware of two pairs of green eyes exchanging a wary glance. Then Aline laughed.

"Poor pickings a thief would have of us!" she declared forthrightly. "We have not a copper tabutz between us."

"Aye," Allyn echoed his sister. "Our father the miller makes a good living, but we've no coin to squander."

Even as they spoke, the town of Eltaba came into view. A prosperous, well-kept town it was, too. Just this side of the town a mill wheel revolved, driven by a swiftly flowing stream.

"Your father's?" Pendravyn asked.

Allyn nodded. The wagon rumbled to a stop in front of the mill. A short, stout little man, his red hair graying, shot like a bee from the mill. He stopped, his eyes widening with fright as he caught sight of the riderless horse. Relief swept his face when he saw young Allyn on the wagon seat.

"S'Lemmia," he bellowed. "S'Lemmia, come quickly! Allyn be hurt!"

Even as he called, a tiny bundle of a woman, shorter than her husband, her brown braid wrapped neatly about her crown, came on flying feet from the miller's cottage. Aline, swinging down from her horse, intercepted her parents.

"Nay, 'tis but a scratch! Mama, Papa, do not fret!"

Allyn climbed down stiffly, his parents buzzing about him with concern.

"Come, come, into the house. How did this happen?" the worried miller asked.

"Bandits," Pendravyn answered briefly. "We came upon these two chicks of yours surrounded by a band of rogues, and thanks to this good knight and his squire, we were able to come to their aid."

"Well come, kind strangers, into our home. We would see you fed and hear more of these troublin' events."

Inside the rambling cottage which sat near the mill, the miller's wife bustled about bringing cold sweet milk and warm slices of new-baked bread, pots of butter and honey and jam to the trestle table, while her husband fussed about Allyn, fetching a cushion for him to sit upon. His sister took her place beside him and Joss marveled at the sight they made. The pair of them, tall and elegant with their green eyes and high cheekbones, their long, slender hands. Beside them, the miller and his wife looked like two plump sparrows loosed among hawks, so different were the children from their parents.

"And Hetta," the miller's wife S'Lemmia inquired, her bright eyes darkened with concern "did you find her well?"

"Oh yes, Mama," Aline dropped a kiss on her little mother's cheek. "Hetta is well and sends her love to you."

Pendravyn looked up sharply at the name, as did his companions all.

"Hetta?" he repeated. "Nurse Hetta, once of the House of Avat'ar?"

Except for the quick indrawn breaths of the twins, complete silence met the wizard's question. Then the miller, his wife, and the twins rushed into speech at once.

Pendravyn held up his hand.

"Peace, good folk! We seek your friend Hetta because we have a dire need for knowledge of the fabled Swords of Avat'ar. They are part of an ancient prophecy, a prophecy that the High Shaman of the Cherdir seeks to fulfill for his own evil ends. He has kidnapped the infant cousin of these brave young men who travel with us. Moreover, he has gained the Alabine Goblet as foretold by the prophecy, and now, it would seem, he is seeking to discover the whereabouts of the Crossed Swords of Avat'ar."

Looking carefully at the mug of milk before him, Allyn asked slowly.

"This shaman and his followers, they would not hurt an old woman?"

"We hoped to reach her first," Pendravyn replied. "It seems we've traveled here ahead of the High Shaman."

"Why hurt Hetta?" Merys put in, "why not kidnap instead the last surviving heirs of the House of Avat'ar?"

Two hands clasped tightly together on the table as the miller and his wife hovered protectively behind the twins. Pendravyn and Merys regarded them with slight smiles upon their faces, while Joss saw the same shock written on his face mirrored on the faces of his brother, his cousin, the knight, and the squire. All at once, the little miller collapsed and sat beside Aline, drawing his wife close by her waist. He heaved a deep sigh.

"When the great plague descended upon the House of Avat'ar and ruin befell that proud family, 'twas believed that all had perished. However, one infant cousin survived. His nurse took him and cared for him when his parents died of the plague. And when in time the young master grew to be a man and took a wife, it came to pass that she bore twins, as was usual in the House of Avat'ar, but of these babes, one saw not the light of day. The parents grieved for the lost child, but were blessed with the child which lived.

"And this young man married when he was grown, and his first-born were also twins, one of which was again stillborn and one son which lived. Not long after his first birthday, both of his parents sickened and died. Then Nurse Hetta took up her charge and left behind the accursed home of the Avat'ar nobles. She brought her charge here, to her own dear kinswoman's cottage and raised the boy herself. When she had grown old and weary, her young master took himself a wife and here, away from the shadow of the House of Avat'ar, the last son and his wife gave birth to a son and a daughter. And as you see here before you, both babes thrived.

"Now it was that Nurse Hetta and all who knew them rejoiced. But this young father decided that the curse was lifted from his noble line and rode off to reclaim his property, leaving his wife and babes in Eltaba. Good Nurse Hetta begged him not to go back, but he was convinced the curse was lifted and he would come to no harm. To the ruins he rode and as he explored them, a viper bit him. He died almost instantly, and here in Eltaba his wife sickened and died within hours of her young husband's death."

"Poor Nurse Hetta!" S'Lemmia sighed. "She nearly went mad with grief! She gave over the babes to my husband and me, and we have raised them like our own."

"We have not dared," Aline told us, her green eyes deepening with emotion, "to return to the House of Avat'ar."

"But," Pendravyn cocked one white brow at her, "you would do so, like your father before you, if you could retrieve the Crossed Swords of Avat'ar?"

"Yes!" Aline and Allyn spoke as one, then Allyn shrugged and winced as the movement pained his side. "But even with our births, both our parents fell victim to the curse. We cannot hope to enter the ruins!"

"Ah, but we can." The knight smiled with a grim determination and patted the hilt of Monsterslayer. "This mighty sword was tempered in magic and in fire! It will take me safely into the ruined House of Avat'ar and out again. All I need," he finished, "is to know where to look for the swords of your honor."

A shiver ran up Joss' spine. They were so close! By tomorrow they might have the swords! The shaman Khasil would have no hope of success. They could free Daniel and take him home!

"Tradition says," Aline supplied soberly, "that the Crossed Swords hung always in the Great Hall. But," she concluded, tossing her head in frustration, "the hall, like the entire house, has fallen to ruin. They cannot hang there still!"

"Perhaps not," Merys ventured. "But we shall never know unless we look." As she spoke she rose and crossed the keeping room to the great hearth. There she drew a pouch from her pocket and withdrew a pinch of a dark green powder that smelled faintly of the deep forest. This she flicked into the fire. The flames flared and burned as deep a green as Allyn's and his twin's eyes. Then in the heart of the flames a black ruin of a house appeared. As the company stared in fascination at this vision, the ruins disappeared and the House of Avat'ar looked as it must have done before ever it was cursed.

Tall towers four stories high flanked a front marked in the middle by a portcullis with its gate closed. Ranks of shuttered windows faced the great building on the top three floors, but the ground floor had a series of high, narrow slits, where archers would have stood if trouble faced the House of Avat'ar. Then the vision led them into the heart of the house until they might have stood in the center of the Great Hall itself.

There, at the far end of the hall stood a high dais upon which were two towering chairs, carved into fantastic shapes and painted white, with the writhing shapes gilded in gold. Above the raised seats of the firstborn twins, glowed two swords. Gems that mirrored the green of the twins' eyes sparkled in the silver tracery of the hilts while the blades bit deeply into finely wrought white leather scabbards. Then the flames flickered darkly about the edges of that vision and in a moment the swords, the Great Hall, the ruins all disappeared. Those in the miller's cottage were left staring once more into an ordinary fire on the grate.

"But, m'lady," Nickolas whispered, "were they real?"

Merys looked at the gathered company and grinned.

"As real as you or I, Master Nickolas. The Crossed Swords of Avat'ar hang yet in the Great Hall, behind the curse. Ours for the taking!"

The Cherdir

Under cover of the falling darkness, Cheruk grunted with satisfaction. His age-sister's soft footfalls told him that Chella approached the water wagon. She fumbled with her buckets, dropping them. Stooping to retrieve one which rolled partly under the wagon, she met her age-brother's eyes without the slightest jerk of surprise.

"*He*," Cheruk could not bring himself to utter the high shaman's name, "plans to cross the river with a hand-picked group of warriors tomorrow, leaving all else camped here. He has ordered our father to move our warriors into position to attack. His prey comes this way with something that the shaman is desperate to possess."

Cailie, drifting like a shadow on Cheruk's thoughts, felt the presence of the goblet like a weight upon her soul—an icy weight like a glacier growing about her, sealing in her essence until soon there would come a time when even thought was denied her. She saw no place for her in this desperate struggle, no way to affect the outcome, no way to insure the safety of Daniel. Only one slim hope kept the weight of the goblet from crushing her spirit into oblivion. In all her other advdentures, no matter what the odds against her and her companions and allies, she had had some small part to play. Since fate had brought her hence, surely there was yet some way in which she could act. She would fight death—the final destruction of her soul—until all hope was gone.

Chella straightened with bucket in hand and set it under the water wagon's spigot.

Cheruk's voice, clearer and strained, reached her.

"Be ready, then, when his attention is drawn elsewhere."

"Here," the gruff voice of a guard sounded beside Chella's stiffened figure. Cheruk froze and flattened himself deeper into the grass and shadows beneath the wagon, not daring to breathe in case a blade of grass should move and betray him. "Let me carry those for you."

CHAPTER ELEVEN

Young Cailie

The hound darted before her and was down the steps ahead of her. Under cover of the thunderous rage erupting in the chamber behind her and the thickness of the wall between, Cailie swung about and ran. With a stitch in her side, she reached the grotto and panted for breath. Where was the hound? Where was her four-footed companion?

A lean shadow detached itself from the shadows of the cavern and Cailie choked back a scream and prepared to flee around the pool. Then the glimmering light from the pool lit up the features of the young man who stood there. Dark eyes glinted in the light, and Cailie's fear melted into relief. Cade! Then he stepped forward, clear of the shadows, and shock, then sudden, irrational anger overflowed within her.

"You!" She hissed.

White teeth gleamed in the briefest of grins, then Pendarek reached out and took her by the arm. He was taller than she remembered, with broader shoulders, and he held himself contained like pooling water stilled and calm. His fair hair grew over his collar and his cheeks and chin were dark with stubble.

"Quietly, sweet Cailie," he cautioned in a low voice. "Will you come with me?"

It was on the tip of her tongue to refuse him. What was he doing here? And, and his eyes, she thought in confusion, then, inconsequentially, where was Cade? She bit her lip painfully and nodded jerkily.

His ferocious grin startled her and something flashed in the depths of his eyes. Those deep eyes so like Cade's.

They went, not by magic, but on foot, back through the ever-narrowing tunnel to the stream and hence to the grove of trees, giving the army's flank a wide berth across the valley to the mountains which held the keep. Cailie followed Pendarek up a rocky hillside until he lay flat on a stone ledge and reached down to pull her up beside him. Breathless and flushed, she blinked with astonishment. An overhang created a shallow shelter at the back of the ledge. The witch Merys knelt by the prone figure of the wizard Pendravyn, his head cradled in her lap.

"I'm not dead yet, young Cailie," the wizard uttered wryly and opened his eyes, grimacing as she flung herself down beside him and grasped his hand. A sudden warmth lit her as her wren talisman glowed brightly from within her pocket. A smile tugged at the corner of the wizard's mouth as he noted the blue light.

Merys spoke, her voice low.

"I have scried within the locked tower of the Black Keep. Alaric, through Bakshir, has drawn power from certain of the objects stolen from the monastery, but he is still searching for that which he needs most—the one thing which will feed the dark power he yearns to unleash. It eats at his soul like a disease that cannot be healed."

Cailie shuddered and felt Pendarek's hand on her shoulder.

Pendravyn moved irritably, frustrated by his physical weakness.

"Alaric, ever impatient even as a child, cannot be counseled much longer to hold off his forces. He is ready to fling open the gates and attack his cousin and the army gathered with the king. Our kind—" he indicated himself, the lady Merys, and Pendarek with a wave, "cannot use our power against the tower.

"You see the red—there—upon the tower walls?"

Cailie looked and another shudder ran through her. The angry cast of those walls seemed to eat at the stone and contaminate the very air round the tower with evil. Pendarek's grip tightened on her shoulder.

"Bakshir has set a spell upon it so that the very walls repel any magic set against them."

"Thus," Merys took up the tale, "we cannot attack directly." At Cailie's quick glance, the witch leaned forward protectively towards Pendravyn; he reached for her hand without looking at her. "We are here, Cailie, and there—" she pointed to the mountain slopes behind the tower, "and there—" she pointed to the other side of the valley. "Our kind. We cannot enter the tower, for none can breach the spell that Bakshir has made. We are here to try and stop whatever power he succeeds in bringing forth."

"If I were stronger," Pendravyn railed, and Merys squeezed his hand with compassion.

"If you were stronger, my love, Bakshir might never have made it this far along his quest for power. But, now," she sighed and did not finish her thought.

Pendarek spoke and Cailie half-turned to see him better. His dark eyes reflected back the pale witch-light his sister had conjured.

"There is this in our favor, Cailie. The spell my sister spoke of—it keeps us out, but it keeps Bakshir within, for he cannot work any magic to spirit himself away unless," he finished with a grimace, "he succeeds in finding that which he seeks."

Pendravyn coughed as he heaved himself onto one elbow.

"He has not yet succeeded, Cailie, because he has not divined the secret of the holy treasure of the monks. These many days, when this accurst illness kept me bound to my bed, the fair lady Merys has been my willing partner and searched out from near and far certain ancient documents for us to study."

And what, Cailie wondered in exasperation, had Pendarek been doing? A light gleamed disconcertingly far back in the depths of his eyes as though he might have read her mind, and Cailie flushed.

"And?" she prompted the wizard.

"The holy treasure of the monastery, we discovered, grew one piece at a time as gifts given to the order of monks out of tribute or piety or in gratitude for grace granted, prayers answered. Over the centuries, certain pieces were sold off or traded away as the monastery's fortunes prospered or declined. But, always, the holiest treasures remained. It is those which Alaric has stolen away with Bakshir, convinced that one among the treasures has a power which Bakshir can control to unleash all the devils of hell." His voice weakened and a coughing fit shook him. Merys eased his shoulders gently down until his head rested in her lap, his eyes burning with fever.

"What we discovered is this, Cailie. There is no one piece among those which make up the treasure which holds the key Bakshir so eagerly seeks. But," she held up a hand to forestall Cailie's question, "what he does not yet understand is that it is the treasure as a whole in which the power is to be found."

Pendravyn's voice came more strongly.

"Remove one piece, any piece, and the power of the treasure will be broken. As long as the treasure is intact, the power remains. Alaric and Bakshir have only to test the treasure as a whole and they will have that which they desire."

Merys' eyes darkened with despair.

"But we cannot pass the bespelled barrier that Bakshir has set upon his tower and if they stumble upon the secret of the treasure's power—." Merys bit her lip.

Cailie's hand flew to the pocket of her jacket where she had thrust the goblet before her headlong flight away from the chamber. The shock of Pendarek's appearance had driven it from her mind. Before she could speak, a high, piercing note sounded below them and the keep's gates were thrown wide. Alaric's army charged forth even as his kinsmen stood their ground next to the king, whose arm was lifted high to hold back those under his command. The gates were cleared, she had time to note, before the king's arm dropped and his men surged forth to engage the enemy with a great roar.

The black tower glowed so fiercely in response to the tumult that it seemed the rock must break into flames. Into this moment of stunned silence, Pendarek spoke quietly, but Cailie heard the emotion rippling in his voice.

"The wren has done what we could not."

Pendravyn heaved himself up again, his incredulous gaze mirrored on the witch's face as he looked from Pendarek to Cailie.

"Tell us," he commanded, his brow furrowing at Cailie's tale. Merys shot her brother an enigmatic gaze, though she held her tongue, when Cailie told of the hound that had sought shelter with her. Her story ended, Pendarek put out a hand to stay her when she would have drawn the goblet from its hiding place.

"Nay, sweet Cailie," he cautioned, "leave it unseen."

Pendravyn nodded and winced, as if the movement pained him. Merys stirred beside him.

"If we do not see that which you have taken, then knowledge of it cannot be forced from us." At Cailie's grimace, the witch stared beyond her brother and gestured at the battle raging in the valley. "We may have broken the power of the treasure thanks to your courage and cleverness, Cailie," she gave Cailie one of her rare smiles, lightning quick, and continued, "and if this battle swings in our favor, the rest of the treasure may yet be recovered and reinstated at the monastery at Rebehan. But it is not certain that we will succeed. Even without the power of the holy treasure, Bakshir calls upon dark forces to aid Alaric's fight."

Pendravyn moved and his blue eyes sought Cailie's. His words came softly.

"It is best, I think, if yon goblet is never restored to its home. The treasure will become just that once more and nothing more—a hoard of beautiful objects that the monks can hedge against hard times, so those for whom they care shall never be in need. Nothing except normal human greed to tempt anyone else to thoughts of theft. And against that, the monks have ample guards."

Pendravyn reached out to grasp Cailie's hand.

"Pendarek will take you hence, Cailie. Go and hide away your purloined treasure. Then home for you and our blessings go with you, child of Caristoke, for once again you have shown yourself to be as brave a warrior as any that the king commands."

Cailie squeezed his hand and blinked back tears. Merys' fingers closed about her amethyst pendant.

"Take her now, Pendarek, while Alaric and Bakshir's attention is focused on the battle below us. I will shield your going as best I may."

Pendarek stood and helped Cailie to her feet. Tears ran blindly down her cheeks as Pendarek wrapped his arms around her. She held on tightly, and even as his arms enfolded her, darkness swallowed them, and the shelter fell away.

Pendravyn

Long before the first faint rays of dawn played about the rough edges of morning, the wizard and his friends were on their way. Aline and Allyn would not be left behind, although they promised the miller and his wife that they would not try to enter the doomed ruins of their ancestral home. Rather, both would wait with the rest of the wizard's party, for only Sir

Daven and Pendravyn planned to pass into the ruins.

Beside his older cousin on the wagon seat, Mykael held fast to the chain from which hung Aelfris' heavy seal.

"We have the '*Barque of Justice*,'" he remarked to Joss, "and soon we'll have the Crossed Swords, too. *He*," the younger boy did not name the high shaman, "has Daniel and that old goblet. Half of the prophecy will lie with us and half with him. So, how do we make him give back Daniel?"

From behind them, a tiny sliver of music was piped upon the cool morning breeze. Looking back, Joss caught Nickolas' grin as he patted his silver piccolo. Well, it had certainly saved the knight from the spell cast over him. Mykael nodded as if the same thought had occurred to him, and struck up a conversation with Allyn, who sat beside them, about the sturdy mountain stallions that his sister Aline and the wizard rode. The lady witch Merys handled Lilly and Imelda as Sir Daven rode before the wagon and Squire Persiflas came along behind on Hesperius.

What bothered Joss, like a nagging earache, was the question of how they were to find the shaman. So far, he'd managed to keep fairly close tabs on them. But where was he now?

That question remained unanswered as the turquoise and yellow wagon and those who rode with it drew closer and closer to the ancient House of Avat'ar. A gloom, chill and damp as fog, seeped into their talk and settled on their faces as they approached the ruins. Skirting the town of Escran, they had seen no one, were accosted by no one, no demons, no grass-mummies, no hired soldiers. Only that deepening sense of gloom rode ever more heavily with them. The road left the sea edge, following the course of a river that wound from the sea at the port of Escran through a forest grown up in lands once tilled at the foot of the castle's hill. Leaving the woods and river behind, they halted below the hill on which the blackened stone blocks of the ruined castle lay tumbled. Pendravyn pulled up his stallion beside the wagon once more. His azure eyes took in the anxious, troubled faces before him. He nodded at the twins.

"Aline and Allyn of Avat'ar, have we thy permission to enter the Great Hall of thine ancestors?"

"By the grace of our Lord, we grant thee entrance," the two chanted as one. "Take up the Crossed Swords at our bequest and deliver our birthright unto us!"

"As thou sayest, so shall it be done." Sir Daven drew the great sword Monsterslayer from its scabbard and touched the blade to his forehead in a salute to Aline and Allyn.

"Be careful, my love," the lady witch's brown eyes flashed as they swept the wizard's lanky form. Pendravyn straightened his turban with a short grin.

"Never fear, Merys! I will tread softly in the House of Avat'ar. Keep your eyes and ears open as you await our return."

Gathering up the reins of the stocky little mountain horse, he urged it forward to join Sir Daven. Moving in unison, they mounted the overgrown trail that led to the ruins above. The rest of the company watched as they reached the first of those dark, tumbled stones. Not even the outline of a tower remained standing. Dismounting, the wizard and the knight scrambled by foot into the center of the ruins without incident. Pendravyn raised his hand before him and light sparked from his fingertips, jumping into the space before him and running like tracery around the outline of a great doorway. Into that arched way he stepped with Sir Daven. As if they were swallowed up into nothingness, they disappeared before the company's eyes.

Aline's sharp intake of breath was followed by Nickolas' gasp and Mykael's startled cry of "No!" Merys reached out a hand to Mykael and hugged both Joss' little brother and his cousin close. Joss held fast to the knowledge that Pendravyn had acted as if he'd known what he was doing. About him the day's bright sunshine dimmed as clouds seemed to grow from the gray gloom that surrounded the ruins.

When at last Joss thought he would scream with despair, that same bright light crackled and cut through the gloom and a second later Pendravyn and the knight came charging into sight. The arched doorway disappeared as soon as they had cleared it. The two men ran for their horses and rode as if pursued towards the wagon, although nothing followed them through that door that any could see. As the wizard and knight drove their mounts recklessly down the trail, the sense of doom grew heavier and thicker about them all. Merys was already turning the wagon back towards town, Lilly and Imelda rolling the whites of their eyes.

"Run!" Pendravyn's cry was lost in the thunder of hooves on the road as Merys gave the mares their heads and let them go at a gallop. The wizard raced alongside the wagon, his eyes fierce as a hunting hawk's. Behind Joss in the wagon, Nickolas and Mykael, faces white and tense, held on for dear life. Then a terrible booming noise bounced off the road before them, throwing up a cloud of dust that settled over the white mares and brought the wagon and its outriders to a standstill as the lady witch Merys clung to the reins and fought to keep the panicked team from overturning the wagon.

"Here!" Pendravyn plucked a slender white scabbard from the waist of his robes and tossed the sword to Aline, who grabbed it and passed it forth to her brother. A second white scabbard sailed after the first and for the first time in generations, the Crossed Swords of Avat'ar were in the hands of the firstborn twins.

The dust cloud darkened and thickened in front of them. Twirling and rising, it took on the shape of a funnel and twisted into their path with deadly intent. Tracing symbols that glowed into life in the air, Pendravyn shouted a spell of slowing that caused the dust cloud to hesitate and spin on its axis. Angrily it spun in place, and then slowly it moved forward one inch at a time as sweat beaded and ran from the wizard's forehead. Back one inch, then forward. Back and forth. How long could the wizard hold off the fury of that wind-driven cloud?

"Run!" The wizard shouted, his voice hoarse from strain. "All of you, into the woods! Scatter!"

The Cherdir

By daybreak, the warriors were mounted and fording the river. Khasil rode in the lead, followed by his packhorses. Chella and Nima rode behind those, the ever-present guard behind them. Cheruk kept to his father's side, his eyes constantly on the look-out for a sign of those whom the shaman sought. The shaman's troop rode some distance from the river into a wooded grove. Here Khasil halted and summoned two of his guards. His white braids twisted in the wind and his cold gaze raked the warriors. He beckoned and the great clan-chief joined him for a short conference.

The Cherdir clan-chief rode among his men, dividing them into those who would ride with him and those who would stay behind in camp. He took with him the most seasoned warriors, but when he paused in front of his son, his right arm shot out and he clapped Cheruk's shoulder. Cheruk urged his mount forward to join the group of warriors who dismounted in the shade and checked their mounts and their gear until the clan-chief gave the order to ride out.

Passing his kinswomen without a glance, Cheruk rode stiffly at the rear of the mounted warriors. Two pairs of dark eyes watched him ride by. Nima and Chella dismounted and made camp with those left behind, although no fires were lit. They sat apart from their Cherdir kinsmen under the watchful eyes of the guard. Men rechecked their mounts and gear and any conversation was carried out in low voices. Chella sat with her knees drawn up to her chin while Nima fed the baby from a skin of milk. He was drowsy and one fat hand waved once or twice as he finished, content and quiet. Their four guards talked among themselves, but their eyes kept going to the path Khasil had taken out of the forested grove. Those men left behind, Chella noted, sat well away from the guards, but they too watched the woods and busied themselves with their mounts and weapons.

Keeping her eyes on the guards, her movements as contained as possible, Chella slid Cheruk's *kerdun* from her boot, along the seam in her breeches, upward inch by achingly slow inch until her hand reached her waist, before she stood in one abrupt movement and thrust the small knife out of sight into the wide leather wrap that encircled her waist. She reached a bundle down from her horse and pulled out the cloths needed to change the babe and wrap him well.

Nima laid the infant on a blanket on the ground as Chella spread the soft changing cloths beside him. His dark eyes watched them both, but he did not cry or make a sound as Nima swaddled him tightly, then bundled him into a pack meant to be slipped across a mother's back. Nima knelt with her back to her age-sister and Chella slipped the pack's strap over her shoulder and settled the precious bundle against the hollow of Nima's back.

As if on cue, they heard a commotion beyond the grove where they awaited the shaman's return—the sound of a horse being ridden hard. Some of the warriors left behind were mounting, the guards rising, when Cheruk dashed wildly into the clearing and pulled up, already turning his horse's head sharply back towards the path from the grove.

"Ambush!" he shouted. "The Cherdir are falling!" And following on his cries came the roar and screams of battle. Nima and Chella mounted in the confusion as the camp was abandoned.

"Go! Go!" Cheruk was screaming. "The Cherdir are falling!"

The guards—warriors themselves until Khasil took them from their families for his personal guards—mounted and followed after their comrades. In that second, Chella acted, bringing her horse close to the pack animal on which the shaman's goods were tied. With the ease of long practice, she whipped her brother's *kerdun* from her waist and sliced open the first chest, cutting its bindings and grabbing the clan-chief's *kerdun.* Cheruk caught it and thrust it into his boot before two of the guards glanced behind, whipped about as one and rode furiously back towards camp, shouting as they did for the other two guards to follow.

"Go!" Cheruk shouted to his sister. "Take the child and go!"

Nima wheeled her horse about and raced for the river, Chella matching her pace for pace.

Cailie watched them go through Cheruk's eyes. Safe, let Daniel be safe! But, here, now, there was still work to be done. Feverishly, Cheruk shoved the packhorse into the path of the oncoming guards, hacking at the ties of the second chest. It came free wrapped in its covering and tumbled to the ground. Turning his surefooted mount, it reared once, and then Cheruk thundered from the clearing—away from his sisters, away from the Cherdir. Risking one backward glance, he saw the shaman's guard split. Two horsemen rode after the women, one retrieved the chest holding the goblet, and the other guard shot out of the clearing after him. Faster, Cailie urged, as if her wish alone could give Cheruk's horse wings.

Nima saw, ahead of her, the shallow banks of the river approaching. She shot a glance behind her and in that moment her horse stumbled and she felt her shoulder wrenched as a hand grasped the bundled child and pulled him from her.

"No!" she screamed and twisted around, but a blur of movement closed in on her left and a second hand reached out to slap her mount hard on the rump as he recovered his footing. Then she was hanging on for dear life, her horse plunging straight into the river, and through her screams of fury, she saw Chella struggling up the bank on the other side. Then she too was across and the two young women fell into each other's arms, bitter weeping loosing their despair. It was Emira who came to them, silently wrapping dry blankets about them, her eyes on the far shore where her husband and her son had disappeared.

Pendravyn

Reaching behind him, Joss half-plucked his brother and cousin from the wagon and pushed them ahead of him, and then he reached up to help Allyn down as his sister aided him from her mount. Sir Daven, Monsterslayer bared, flanked Pendravyn, while the squire struggled to take the reins from Merys and free her to help the wizard.

As Joss cast one quick glance behind him, he saw the dust cloud burst into flames and out of that fire rode a mass of fierce warriors. Aline drew forth her sword, the silver blade slicing at the air. A vine whipped about Joss' face in that instant and he stumbled half to his knees. Ahead of him, Nickolas and Mykael ran on without looking back. Joss' cry went unheard in the noise all about them. Freeing himself, he struggled on. Casting another terrified glance behind him, he saw his friends fighting for their lives. Hesitating for a moment—his little brother and Mykael were somewhere ahead of him—he half-turned back, should he follow or try to help those who fought? A trio of mounted warriors wheeled in his direction. Blind panic seized him then, and he had wits enough to think only that they must not find Mykael and Nickolas as he bolted away from the path the two boys had taken as fast as he was able.

Bruised and cut by sharp tree branches, Joss ran on and on until he had no more breath to run and collapsed under a bush, waiting for some ruffian to seize him and drag him from his hiding place. After several moments he caught his breath and realized that no one was near. He had slipped away from his pursuers in the woods. But, where was he? And, more importantly, where were his friends and Nickolas and Mykael?

Gathering up his strength and his courage, Joss shimmied up a low-branching tree and scanned the scene that appeared in the valley below. Trees lay uprooted where the twisting dust cloud had rampaged. Lying across the road on its side was the wizard's turquoise and yellow wagon. His heart lurched in his chest. Where were his friends? Two of Khasil's warriors worked to upright the wagon. From the woods, two others appeared, leading Imelda and Lilly, who tossed their heads and reared in a vain effort to break free.

But, there! Into the middle of the road paced a tall, gaunt figure. Dressed all in black, he had close-cropped black hair, except for long thin white braids which swung on either side of his face. Hands behind his back, he paced to and fro in front of two young people—Aline and Allyn, the latter holding his side while his sister held him. On the ground at their feet lay a third figure. A rough blindfold hid her eyes, and her hands and feet were bound. Merys!

Dazed, Joss watched as Khasil—for surely the man with the close-cropped black hair, white braids swinging about his face, was the shaman himself—directed his men to put Merys' still figure into the righted wagon. Aline helped Allyn climb in, and then two of the Cherdir horsemen joined them. Khasil mounted a tall red, rawboned horse and headed south along the road away from Escran. After a long while Joss found himself climbing down from his perch. Despair settled over him. Pendravyn! Tears choked him. They must have died in that battle—Pendravyn and Sir Daven and Squire Persiflas. For alive, Pendravyn would never have suffered Merys to have been taken captive. And how was he to find Nickolas and Mykael? Had they—he gulped and finished the terrible thought—had they perished or did they yet live? Were they as alone as he? Were they hurt?

Rubbing his knuckles against his eyelids as tears slipped down his cheeks, Joss gulped them back and stumbled along until he came to a thin trickle of a stream where he took a long drink and splashed water over his hot, tear-streaked face to cool off. Taking a deep breath, he tried to think what he should do next.

Alone, on foot, how could he ever hope to find his brother and his cousin? Without thinking, Joss clutched at his dragon pin and fought back a fresh attack of tears. Maybe he could summon up a little of the courage of Otaghi-Ray—long enough at least to help himself and find those he loved, for he refused to believe that they had perished. Holding fast to that thought as if it were indeed a lifeline, Joss struggled on through the trees in the direction he thought Mykael and Nickolas had taken. His path brought him at last into a small clearing at the edge of a bluff. There was no sign of anyone else. Hopelessly, he dropped to his knees and shut his eyes tight against his fear.

"Oh, Otaghi-Ray!" Joss groaned and covered his face with his hands, "if only you could help me now!"

How long he knelt in that clearing, Joss could never recall exactly. It might have been hours or only moments when a faint breeze whipped through the grass beneath him and set the leaves to dancing on the trees behind him. Head bowed, sunk in misery, the forlorn boy paid no attention as the wind increased, then stopped abruptly.

"You are frightened, little dragon-brother," a deep, rusty roar of a voice purred above him. "How can I help you?"

Opening his eyes, delirious with joy, Joss stared at the magnificent deep pink dragon that hovered beyond the cliff edge. Little puffs of smoke escaped his nostrils and his mouth as he spoke, but the black eyes that held the boy's own were full of kindness.

"Otaghi-Ray!"

"I heard your call, little brother," the dragon rumbled. "Again and again, you have been willing to sacrifice your life for the lives of your kinsmen and your friends. How could I ignore your peril when we two are dragon-brothers?"

This time, tears of relief sprang to Joss' eyes. Words tumbled from his lips.

"Khasil, the Cherdir shaman, has kidnapped my baby cousin, and he has the Alabine Goblet, too. We found Aelfris' ship and the Crossed Swords of Avat'ar, but . . ." Joss' voice broke for a moment, "but Khasil attacked

us. Now he has Aline and Allyn with the
Swords of Avat'ar and the lady witch Merys!

"I lost Nickolas and Mykael and . . ."
Speech failed him. He could not put into words
the fate of the wizard and the knight and
squire.

The great eyes blinked and Otaghi-Ray
landed on the bluff edge.

"Are you certain that the old one has
perished? Did you see his mount in the hands
of the evil one's warriors?"

Hope shocked Joss into utter silence. Rex
the Warhorse had been nowhere in sight
among the High Shaman's troops. Nor was that
cantankerous brown-eyed, blue-eyed mule,
Hesperius! His heart pounded. There had been
no sign, either, of the surefooted, sturdy
mountain stallion the wizard had been riding.
Surely, they must live!

"Come, little brother," Otaghi-Ray's long
neck shimmered like the under-side of a rose
as he dipped it towards the boy, "let us soar
above the earth and see if we can find your lost
companions."

A gentle puff of smoke warmed him as Joss
climbed onto the scaled back of the dragon. It
was hard and firm and alive with sparkles of
light and color. The triangular face sought his
own.

"Fear not, Joss dragon-heart! You will not fall. In which direction does this Khasil flee? For surely the old one shall follow to free the lady witch."

Seated between Otaghi-Ray's powerful shoulders, a sense of strength flowed through Joss, and he tried to remember what the knight had told them. Of the black tower of Ma'al from whence the dark wind flew, seeking its sister city, Ka'ma-atl. This lay in ruins in the Southern Wastes. But what had the prophecy said?

"*The Barque of Justice shall sail upon the Holy River, the Crossed Swords of Avat'ar held above the Alabine Goblet as the reborn child of Ma'al drinks.*" The words made no sense, for even now they did not know where to find this Holy River. The Southern Wastes were a vast, nearly lifeless desert. No rivers had flowed there as long as anyone could remember. Only shifting sands could mark the tumbled, ruined streets of Ka'ma-atl.

Otaghi-Ray's powerful muscles surged, his wings outspread, and boy and dragon were launched into the sky. As though he had read Joss' mind, and perhaps he had, Otaghi-Ray headed south. With each beat of his outstretched wings, hope coursed through Joss. The dragon's heart beat as his. The two might have been one being aloft in the air, so much a part of the ancient dragon did the boy feel.

Below him the low hills bordering the gentle plains of Eltaba appeared. Ranged beyond the foothills, a tall, black line of saw-toothed, snowcapped mountains towered oppressively. On the other side of those forbidding mountains, the Southern Wastes stretched as far as one could see.

Then, in a high pass leading up into the mountains, a line of tiny, moving specks caught Joss' eye. As he jabbed a finger, the scaled dragon banked and swooped lower. With a farsight unknown to him in normal times, Joss found that he could make out the procession as it climbed higher and higher into the mountains. Angry puffs of smoke escaped from his dragon-brother as Joss identified the thin, black-robed shaman and behind him, the wagon with its captives. All about these central figures rode Khasil's horsemen. Where was the wizard? Where was Pendravyn?

Otaghi-Ray swung higher once again and this time circled over the crests of the mountains. Below him the desert wastes reflected back the glare of the sun. The only break in that heat-filled plain was a black spot. As the dragon and rider drew closer, the darkened area was revealed as the spill of ruined, abandoned streets and buildings that marked Ka'ma-atl. Otaghi-Ray flew well clear of that area. It seemed to draw in the heat around it and send it out again with a cold, dank chill. No one moved among those ruined streets and no one moved on the sands of the Southern Wastes. The dragon headed back to the mountains.

Then Joss' breath caught in a gasp. As if he could see beneath those restless sands, a snaking, crawling stone river wound through the wastes. Another joined it, then another. Like a braided river system, only of stone. Dry and buried beneath the sands! Once full of water—long before the memories of anyone now living in this world, rivers had flowed to the city of Ka'ma-atl. And there, where all the winding tributaries flowed into the mighty trunk—the Holy River itself!

With a sudden movement that caused Joss to hang on tighter, Otaghi-Ray dipped and swung in a wide circle away from the direction in which Khasil approached the wastes. Back over the mountains he soared, circling ever lower and lower. A wild cry of joy escaped the rider on his back. A ragged, scraggly group rode single file through a narrow pass.

Pendravyn led the way on his borrowed mount, Nickolas clinging like a monkey to his back. Behind him followed Hesperius, carrying the squire and Mykael. Sir Daven brought up the rear on Rex, the black charger's hooves thundering on the rough track. Otaghi-Ray flew lower and lower until at last Pendravyn caught sight of the dragon and halted his party. Otaghi-Ray settled gently to earth.

"Joss!" Nickolas and Mykael cried out together as he waved, slipped from his perch, and ran to his friends.

"He's ahead of us!" Joss shouted as he ran. "Khasil's ahead of us and he's got Aline and Allyn and the Crossed Swords!"

Pendravyn smiled a crooked grin and held up a hand.

"Ah, but we have retrieved that which makes us equal. The High Shaman of the Cherdir may have the Alabine Goblet and the Swords of Avat'ar, true, but we have the Ship of Justice, and," here he stopped as Rex stepped up beside the wizard and halted, "the child!"

Sir Daven pulled aside the cloak he wore to reveal a round-eyed stare that curved into a grin as the baby's eyes met his eldest cousin's.

"Daniel!" Joss cried out and his baby cousin gurgled and stretched out his arms.

CHAPTER TWELVE

Young Cailie

Cailie felt the darkness lift and heard no sounds of battle, but Pendarek did not loosen his embrace and for one long moment she stood sheltered within his arms. At last she stepped back and met his gaze—those dark, depthless eyes.

"Why did you hide, Pendarek?" she whispered. "Why a mask? Why couldn't you tell me that you were Cade?"

He reached out a hand, but stopped short of touching her. A short, rueful laugh escaped him.

"It was safer that way. There are those who know us well by sight—my sister and our kind, sweet Cailie. To move openly and freely, I took the guise of one beneath notice—one fit only to care for the hounds."

"Then why," she began, stuttering to a stop. "But everyone in camp—."

"I have been the houndsman's assistant before, Cailie," was all he said, but a brief grin sent waves of light sparkling in his eyes. He gave an odd sigh. "It was safer that way," he repeated, although he did not specify aloud for whose safety he had hid himself from her.

Taking her by the arm, he urged her forward. "Let us see what kind of place this is."

They were standing, as far as Cailie could tell, in an immense plaza. Or what had once been a plaza, for the paved surface was cracked and broken, heaved apart as if the ground beneath had buckled violently. Twisted and stunted trees thrust their way through some of the cracks and weeds and grasses were rampant. Around the edges of the open space were great mounds of rubble that must once have been towering structures. At intervals between these, gaps marked where broad avenues had radiated out from this center.

"Which way, fair Cailie?"

She frowned.

"You have the magic, Pendarek." Her voice was harsher than she intended and she cleared her throat. "What is this place?"

His somber gaze measured the bleak ruins about them.

"Za'Matl —a city so long in ruins, its origins and people are legend only." With a sidelong glance at his companion, he continued gently. "I did not bring us to this place, Cailie. You did with the treasure you carry." He gripped her by the shoulders and faced her away from him.

"Look carefully, Cailie," his breath tickled her ear as he turned her about slowly. "Which way?"

She stared into the ruins, helplessness rising within her as Pendarek swung her around. Then she stiffened and her arm rose to point at a narrow gap between two mounds of rubble.

"There."

Pendarek clasped her hand and did not let go as they clambered together over blocks and around and through the wild tangle of bushes and trees. She was breathing heavily when they paused before the gap. Her glance swept up to lock with Pendarek's.

"You won't leave me?"

For answer he squeezed her hand tightly and they set off side by side.

Their going was easier here, as if the narrow way had kept out the light and discouraged the rampant growth in the open plaza, but it was colder, too, as if warmth had never lingered here. Cailie shivered. They reached a small square and here the mounds were smaller. Nerves jumping, Cailie's free hand closed about the wren as she surveyed the ruins about them. The wren was neither warm nor cold to her touch, as her gaze swept the west side of the square. West? It seemed right, though the wren gave no clue, and she nodded in that direction. Partial walls had survived here and she and Pendarek made their way carefully within. Cailie halted and the warmth of Pendarek's hand in hers was all that kept her from bolting, for the chill in this place threatened to sap all life from her.

"There!" Her eyes made out a carved form in one of the battered blocks. Pendarek tugged his hand free and answered her unspoken question.

"I must wait here. I will not leave you, Cailie."

Hesitantly, one forced step after another, Cailie approached that stone face. For face it was, human in cast, but remote and austere as a judge who held no human mercy or kindness. A shallow basin was hollowed out at the base of the carving. As Cailie stood before it, the cold wrapped around her, enveloping her. As it did so, a voice as remote and cold as she felt rang in her mind.

"Thou doth stand before Ka'atl. I who am the voice of the universe, I who have been undisturbed for all time immeasurable. I shall enfold thee, usurper, into the cold void of the universe from which there can be no escape."

"No, no!" Cailie protested and her fingers closed upon the goblet in her pocket. "Please,

no! I came not to disturb, but to bring a gift!"
She held out the goblet with shaking hands.
"Take it! Take it!"

As she held her breath and waited, she was
aware that the inexorable swirling of cold
about her had halted. That vast searching
awareness which was the spirit of Ka'atl
channeled through the stone carving, focused
on the goblet clasped in her trembling fingers.
Like a sigh, she heard the cold voice once
more.

"Place the Alabine goblet, that which once
brought offerings of sweet wine to please me,
into the niche and I shall relent."

With shaking hands Cailie laid the
translucent goblet—it had chased golden
handles and foot—she noticed in that brief
instant—carefully within the basin.

"It is done. Thou art free, but for this: the
mark of Ka'atl lifts from thee so long as thy gift
shall lie here undisturbed."

The cold receded as the voice faded from
her mind, and when it had lifted completely,
Cailie's knees gave out. She would have fallen
had Pendarek not reached her in one long
stride to catch her in his arms.

They stared at the basin holding the goblet
as it sank within the stone carving.

"Quickly, now, let us be gone from this place." At Pendarek's words, the world swung once more around Cailie. When the spinning stopped, she stood in the shadows of the church where she had been kneeling with her grandmother—a lifetime ago, it seemed to her now.

Pendarek's face was hidden in the shadows, and still Cailie did not let go of him. She gripped him tighter as her face twisted and she whispered.

"Damn you, Pendarek, or Cade, or whoever you choose to be!" Reaching up, she pulled his face to hers and kissed him hard upon the mouth, spun on her heel, and ran across the square towards Maily's Cottage.

Pendarek smiled crookedly, one finger at his lips.

"Ah, my sweet Cailie!" he breathed, "when next we meet, we shall not be parted again."

Cailie reached her grandmother's gate and glanced back, in spite of herself. He was gone. She went in by the gate and was surprised to see her mother waiting on the stoop. Wordlessly, her mother opened her arms and gathered her second daughter close. "Come in, child, and weep if you must. Then you can tell me who it is who grieves you so and why."

Pendravyn

Having settled himself in his oldest cousin's arms, Daniel held to Joss with both hands and would not be moved again. Thus, Joss found himself surrounded by his companions.

"You have seen Khasil?" Pendravyn demanded.

"Yes." Joss went on to describe the scene he'd witnessed, Otaghi-Ray's arrival, and the glimpse of Khasil's party climbing through these same mountains.

"How did you escape the whirlwind?" Joss asked his own eager questions. "And how did you find Squire Persiflas?" He shot his brother a quick grin. Nickolas' brown eyes were dancing and his mouth bit back an answering grin. Joss knew that look of old. Nickolas was bursting with excitement and a story to be told as he kept exchanging looks and giggles with Mykael. "And Mykael," Joss asked, "and, of course," he squeezed Daniel, who sat alert but quiet in his arms, "Daniel himself?"

"The first part I can answer," Sir Daven replied. "At Pendravyn's command, I sent my mighty warhorse away from the shaman's forces, but I grabbed this ancient one's bridle as I went and dragged him to safety in spite of himself." The wizard muttered and threw his friend a dark look. Sir Daven winked, but his heart wasn't in it, and Joss could tell he was wishing he'd been able to save Merys from the clutches of the shaman.

"And I can answer for myself," Squire Persiflas took up the tale. "My balky mule, when I would have led him into the fray, all of a sudden galloped like a mindless beast into the heart of the woods. I could not stop or turn him try as I might, the stubborn creature, until at last he halted of his own will, put down his thick head and chewed on a scrubby thistle bush. There I dismounted and tried verily to coax him back to the road, but he would not be budged no matter how I yelled, er, that is, no matter how I persuaded him."

"That's when we heard him—the squire, I mean," Nickolas put in.

"Yeah," Mykael joined the tale. "Nickolas and I ran, just like Pendravyn said, until we were out of breath and had to stop. We hid under some bushes."

"And then," Nickolas' arms were going like a hummingbird's wings, "then we heard a baby crying."

"So," Mykael continued, "we crawled to the edge of the bushes and peeked out."

"There was a sort of camp," Nickolas explained. "A man was pacing back and forth in front of this tree, complaining all the time to another soldier."

"And, hanging from the tree, in a backpack, was Daniel! He knew we were there, Joss, because he looked right at where we were hiding and he never cried again!"

"Yeah," said Nickolas. "I played a little whistle on my piccolo," he patted his pocket, "and the guards sat down in a heap against a tree and closed their eyes."

"Then I," his cousin piped up, "I slipped from our hiding place and tiptoed into the clearing behind the guards, and over to the tree. I unhooked Daniel from the tree limb, put on the backpack, and took off into the trees, circling around to Nickolas."

"We ran as fast as we could away from that clearing," Nickolas finished, "until finally we stopped to rest and that's when we heard Squire Persiflas and Hesperius."

"And I," Pendravyn didn't even look angry anymore, "I led the knight toward an old trail through the hills, to follow Khasil, when we came upon the squire and his precious charges.

"And now," the wizard's eyes flashed, "our tale is told. May we get on with the chase? Khasil, at last count, has half of what he needs, plus. . . ." his husky voice faltered.

"Plus a bargaining chip—the lady Merys," Sir Daven finished for his old friend.

"Fear not, O Graybeard!" Otaghi-Ray spoke for the first time. "Your pace is swift, your cause righteous! You shall not come too late to help her!"

"But Pendravyn," Joss smacked his brow as he remembered, "we know something he doesn't! We know where the Holy River runs!"

"What?!" A chorus of startled voices met that statement.

"'Tis true," Otaghi-Ray's deep voice rumbled. "From on high the pattern of an ancient river system shows beneath the sands of the Southern Wastes. Into one main trunk flowed all the smaller streams, and into the heart of Ka'ma-atl flowed this mighty river!"

"Khasil couldn't possibly see it," Joss announced forcefully.

"No," the old wizard agreed. "But I think it matters not. Some dark force from the city before us feeds the shaman's spells with unusual power and draws him too into the wasted city—to its heart, you may be certain— to the Holy River. There we must go to confront him."

Looking round the shabby band of companions, Joss saw no fear, only determination and acceptance on all faces.

Having recovered Daniel alive and well, Mykael and Nickolas and he had achieved their goal. If they asked, Pendravyn would send them home now, out of the perilous battle to come. But Joss could see written plainly on his brother's small face and Mykael's clenched jaw, the same will as his own—to follow their friends in their quest to end this strange threat to their world and to free Merys and Allyn and Aline from the shaman's clutches.

Mounted before the knight, Daniel now sound asleep in his pack against his cousin's chest, Joss watched Otaghi-Ray soar into the clouds that obscured the highest peaks. They had little to worry them from Khasil's soldiers with the mighty lord of the Fenmarsh as their ally. Onward the wizard and his company rode, cresting the pass and beginning the swift descent onto the broad, arid plain known as the Southern Wastes.

The sun blazed upon them, baking the dry earth around them in a land that never knew the change of seasons. All year round it lay desolate and barren of life. They followed trails that could have been abandoned only yesterday, so little had been their disturbance from humans or natural forces in time unaccountable. On and on the wizard drove them and their mounts, and the nearer they drew to the dark beacon that was Ka'ma-atl, the greater the unease among them. For a high, keening sound, faint at first, grew stronger as their party approached the ruined city. Like the wind thrusting bare winter branches against the side of a house, the sound scraped along their nerve ends, made all the more eerie by the fact that only their horses' hooves stirred up the sands. No wind whistled in the Southern Wastes.

In the distance a scrim of dust rose and fell. Khasil's party paralleled the wizard's own, seeking the source of that moan, that high-pitched whine of frustration that marked the ancient soul of Za'Matl's sister city. Pendravyn appeared not to have noticed them, but Joss saw the strain of his arms as if he would urge his mount to greater efforts by will alone.

The Cherdir

Cailie heard the wren's shrill cry and saw the arrow flying at Cheruk, but there was no warning she could give the young horseman. The arrow took him in the shoulder, and he slumped forward, but still it took both guards to drag him from his horse and bind him. Cheruk's dark eyes burned with fear and frustration, but though they bound his hands and led him back to camp a prisoner, one tiny thought of comfort warmed him, and Cailie, too, although he did not know it. The guards had taken Cheruk's weapons, but they had not thought to search him. The clan-chief's *kerdun* lay hidden still in his boot.

Tight-lipped, his guards rode back into camp and pulled up in alarm, exclaiming. Cheruk, through a haze of pain, stared in puzzlement. The other two guards lay stretched out in the shade of a tree, fast asleep. The cries of their comrades roused them as they demanded to know what had happened. Dazed, the guards left behind whirled about, shouting that the child was right there—had been right there. With loud cries of consternation they joined the other two guards to search the grove about them for the child. Cheruk grunted with satisfaction even as he slid white-faced from his horse. The babe must have been taken from Chella and Nima, but now the child—like Cheruk's age-sisters— was gone. Cheruk slid into welcome oblivion as the pain of his wound claimed him.

His wound bound up and his hands tied to his pommel, Cheruk rode behind his father. The Cherdir warriors had returned, their stern faces grim and set in the face of the forces which Khasil had unleashed. The shaman had ridden into his temporary encampment furious by the loss of the child, but the goblet remained and he had secured that which made his mad laughter ring throughout the camp, causing the horses to rear and roll their eyes and the men to gaze at their fellow warriors uneasily. Two white scabbards hung from the shaman's saddle, and three prisoners rode with them: a lady with auburn hair and two young men alike enough to be twins. A woven leather strap, twisted yellow through black, lay tightly about the woman's neck. This writhed as if alive, but the woman rode with her head high, her features cold, and showed no fear by look or cry. 'And she would not,' Cailie thought with grim satisfaction, for the lady Merys had courage aplenty and the warriors who rode beside her might have saluted her honor and her dignity as befitting one of the Cherdir had not Khasil rode among them.

They ate as they rode out of camp, away from the river and into the hills, for Khasil pushed them hard into the mountains. Time seemed to have no meaning or measure as they rode, and at last they came down out of the mountains onto a dry plain. Here Khasil halted, struck his shaft upon the ground, once, twice, before a sudden spurt of water flowed. The horses were led to drink and waterskins filled at once. They mounted within minutes and rode on.

Cheruk's father held his horse up a moment's pace and fell back beside his son. His eyes met those of Cheruk, who felt a wild impossible hope course through him. There was a spark of awareness in his father's eyes again. The great clan-chief, his *kerdun* no longer held by the high shaman, was escaping the hold of Khasil at last.

'*What,*' Cailie thought, '*what is it that I can do here?*' For though Daniel was now lost to the Cherdir shaman, where was the babe? Merys' power was held in check by the twisted leather thong about her throat, the Alabine goblet rode with the shaman, and with it, those two swords he had taken in battle. Closer and closer, the Cherdir rode towards that which drew forth the cold from the goblet until Cailie thought that her very thoughts would freeze, shatter, and she would be no more. For the wren's song slowed, slowed, and the rose scent was frozen and came no more.

Out of the dry plain, a dead city rose. The ruins of a dead city. Cailie fought off the cold now with every ounce of strength that she could summon. Of course there was a city. Like a twin to that other, the one to which she had come with Pendarek so long ago, this city lay in ruins. The Cherdir shaman rode surefooted through the ancient streets as if some knowledge worked through him. Cailie felt Cheruk gathering his strength, making ready for whatever opportunity might present itself.

Now the hooves of the mounts of Pendravyn's party rang out hollowly on broken cobbled streets. The noise was thrown back at them, magnified by the total silence of the long-dead city. The ruined blocks lay tumbled like common chimney bricks along the street they traveled. As they rode farther into Ka'ma-atl, the roughly cobbled street broadened into a wide, smoothly paved avenue across which a pale sheen of sand flowed before the riders. The high pitched whine had stopped completely and now a fine, stinging wind blew the sand away from the street into a mist of dust that settled over their clothes, their horses, their exposed skin. Joss pulled his *qhahesa* more securely about Daniel to protect the baby's tender skin. The very air held a tremendous sense of waiting, of listening, of command. Gripped by the pull of the city, it seemed to Joss that he and his companions could not leave at this point if they tried.

The street ended abruptly. Sand dunes swirled ahead of them. As the wind ceased to blow as suddenly as it had begun, the dust clouds settled. There! On the opposite side of the sand dunes the street continued. And there, facing them—Khasil, the High Shaman of the Cherdir! Silently he rode onto the sands and halted his big red horse. The white braids swung at either side of the forbidding, sharpened features of that face. Dark eyes burnt with a black intensity that pinned down those arrayed against him with an unrelenting sense of cold anger and frustration.

At some signal Joss could not see, a small group of the Cherdir rode forth, flanking the yellow and turquoise wagon. Pendravyn sat his stallion without sound, tense as they watched two Cherdir horsemen prod Allyn and Aline from the wagon. When the twins stood before the shaman, he raised his hand. A third man strode forth and placed a crystal goblet, its fluted sides translucent, on the ground before the twins.

"Raise thy swords!" The harsh, grating order issued from Khasil. The twins flinched, their faces strained and white, but both lifted their arms until the gleaming Swords of Avat'ar caught the light like fire and crossed above the goblet. The light flickered and flared, glowing red and running like liquid flames that dripped into the Alabine Goblet. As the goblet filled, its fiery contents smoked and flamed.

Joss' arms tightened convulsively about Daniel, now awake, who tilted his wide eyes up to his cousin's face.

"Over my dead body," Joss promised in a fierce whisper, remembering the words of the prophecy.

"Conjure the ship, dog-wizard!" Khasil commanded, pointing a long, black-clad arm at Pendravyn. "Hand over the child of Ka'atl!"

Before Joss, Nickolas' worried face gazed up at him as Pendravyn shook his head.

"We refuse!"

The shaman signaled to his men. A single rider approached, leading another horse. And, on that horse rode the lady witch Merys, hands tied behind her back, eyes blindfolded. The horseman pulled her roughly from her mount and pushed her none too gently beneath the Crossed Swords of Avat'ar. The red fire ran down the sword blades and enveloped the witch like a prison. She stood erect, back ramrod straight.

"Be easy, my love," she called. "Stand fast! And do not obey!"

Rex whickered in challenge and stamped his hooves as the knight's visor rang down. Hesperius moved up beside Joss. From the corner of his eye Joss saw Mykael's hand tightly grasping the Ship of Aelfris. The red fire that played about the witch flared about her feet until the sand ran in molten rivulets. A sudden breeze kicked up about them, and in that moment, Joss remembered Otaghi-Ray and looked up just as everyone about him exploded into action.

Squire Persiflas shifted Hesperius and grabbed Joss and Daniel with him, free from Rex's back as Sir Daven, Monsterslayer flashing, charged forward. The wizard slipped from his horse even as the squire kneed the mule and grabbed for the reins. Joss slid into the saddle behind Nickolas. Then a high, rumbling hiss broke into the melee, shooting flames in every direction as Otaghi-Ray flew into the fray, scattering Khasil's warriors like chaff flying from a tossed and shaken basket.

Raising his hands before him, Pendravyn stood in the midst of the tumult, his hands tracing patterns in the air that glowed with the familiar light that had always marked the wizard's power.

Khasil countered, weaving with his fingers signs and symbols red-hot and strong. For, try as he might, Pendravyn could not break the prison that held Merys, but neither did the fires rise above the sand to consume her. All around the boys, the spirit of the ancient city could be felt, hungry to come out of time, to be loosed into the world again. Its spirit had been dead eons and eons, yet not set free, held to the land of the living by the promise of a prophecy that Ka'ma-atl and Za'Matl might live again.

Cailie watched, as if her soul were a wave of water slowly freezing solid, the shaman Khasil plant the goblet on the ground. Above it, swords crossed over the witch Merys and red fire framed her, dripping from the swords into the Alabine goblet. Pendravyn sat astride his mount as implacable as stone, and there, riding with him, four whose hearts ran with her own blood—Joss stout-heart, protecting the innocent Daniel, Mykael, close-faced and thoughtful, and sweet Nickolas. Nickolas, Nickolas, merry as a piper in the summertime, she thought. *'How I love you all, my boys.'* But the cold bit deeper and deeper into that which was Cailie's spirit, as if magnified by Za'matl's sister city. There would be no good-byes for her nephews. Even as the cold deepened, Cailie's attention was drawn back to the lady Merys. The witch's eyes widened, and Cailie realized, *'She has seen me—she knows I'm here.'* Then, *'Take it, lady Merys,'* she thrust the thought at the witch, *'take the last ounce of strength left to me and push at the bonds that hold you captive, push harder.'* At her thought, a sweet piping filled the air and the witch's foot moved as the cold about Cailie solidified with horrifying finality and the world about her grew black and still.

Sir Daven engaged the horsemen guarding the shaman and his captives, while Otaghi-Ray splintered and divided the greater force of warriors. It was then that Cheruk, his bonds loosened by his father, jerked the great chief's *kerdun* from its hiding place and thrust it at his father. His father swung the *kerdun* in a circle above his head and gave a resounding shout. All around them, the Cherdir warriors spun their mounts about to answer that battle cry.

"To me!" the clan chief commanded. "Hold!" As one, his warriors fell into stillness behind him.

Before them, Pendravyn and Khasil faced each other while Aline and her brother stood frozen, Crossed Swords wielded in the shape of the prophecy. Then Nickolas stirred and a sharp, sweet sigh of music cut through the noise. The wizard's symbols strengthened, flaring into bright life almost too much to bear looking upon. The lady witch strained visibly against her bonds, her eyes widening suddenly as if in sharp surprise. Nickolas piped a quick series of notes and Merys' foot moved. A half-step, another toe's length. Pendravyn's voice rose as his chant led the music of the piccolo. Merys' foot flashed and the Alabine Goblet rolled on its side, spilling out the fury it contained.

Joss' heart eased back into his chest. Now, at last, no more need for Daniel, not with that goblet's vile contents gone! As the goblet fell, so did the crossed swords. Merys' prison flames puffed out and Aline cut the witch's bonds as Allyn fell heavily to his knees. The witch ripped the braided cord from her neck and threw it upon the smoking remnants of the goblet's spilled contents. The squire urged Hesperius to the twins, leading Allyn's mountain stallion. Aline helped her brother stand; he clung to his horse's bridle for support.

Khasil's magic still glowed in the air between himself and the wizard.

"Thou art beaten," Pendravyn shouted. "Give up thy quest and lead thy people back to the Jashtar Mountains."

In reply Khasil spoke other spells and his red symbols stretched and grew, towering above the wizard. Before anyone had time to react, Mykael slipped from Hesperius' back without warning, the squire reaching too late to stop him. Pulling the amulet from his neck as he ran, Mykael stopped short between the high shaman and Pendravyn.

"The ship! The ship! I must have the ship!" Khasil's long, greedy hands struck at Mykael. But the young boy was quicker, jumping aside and laying the chain across his outstretched hands. Khasil gave a howl of madness.

"Let he who is filled with the light of truth take the *Hælvedda* from my hands! For thus is thy ordeal! He who gave it unto me, he who commanded the Ship of Justice in life as well as in death, let Aelfris and his ship judge thee now!"

Stern and unflinching, Mykael stood his ground, the heavy gold amulet catching the light, gleaming like a living being. Eagerly Khasil grabbed at the chain. As his hands closed about the metal, his face twisted, a cry splintering into a thousand fragmented pieces as he screamed. That scream echoed and bounced throughout the dead city of Ka'ma-atl as though the souls of those who had once lived there all cried out at once. Covering Daniel's ears against his chest, Joss held Nickolas close. As the last echoes of that scream faded to a moan, the world righted itself once more and Khasil was only a shabby old man on his knees in the sand, blubbering and crying.

Then Joss caught his breath as Pendravyn reached slowly for that chain. Almost his fingers touched it, and then he stepped back.

"M'love, if you would."

Merys left her place at Allyn's side and faced Mykael.

"Little warrior, you have served the king well. His ship has come in its proper time and to its proper place, for thus was its purpose—to judge the final outcome of this ancient prophecy. Now at last Ka'ma-atl and Za'Matl may rest in peace."

Surprised, Joss saw that this was true. No menace came from the city around him. Even as he looked about, it held no more than cold stone blocks, nothing more. His attention was dragged back to the sight before him. Merys knelt in the sand before his cousin, who gently placed the chain about her neck. The amulet showed proudly against her robes. Nothing happened; no pain twisted her beautiful features. The prophecy was truly ended.

CHAPTER THIRTEEN

Pendravyn

The deep pink neck arched as the glistening black eyes regarded Joss.

"You have retrieved your lost nestling," Otaghi-Ray's voice rumbled, wisps of smoke drifting from his nostrils. "I salute you, my dragon-brother! May your courage never fail! I will keep your image forever in my heart, little warrior! Farewell until we meet again!"

Unfurling his wings, the great pink dragon rippled his muscles and lifted his wings to the sky. Daniel bunched his fingers.

"Bye! Bye!" He rolled his eyes at his older cousin, and Joss grinned.

"You ham, Daniel! Wait until you're old enough to talk. No one will believe you've seen a dragon!" Then his attention was caught by the knight and squire as they approached his cousin. Pendravyn followed Mykael's sad glance to Khasil.

"Nay, child. Do not trouble yourself for this old man. Watch now." The wizard raised his hand and waved at the shaman. A pale light covered the shaman's kneeling form. Pendravyn waved once more and the haze disappeared, leaving the shaman lying on the ground.

"Never fear," Pendravyn hastened to reassure the boy. "I have given him the gift of deep sleep. The Cherdir will take that one home to the Jashtar Mountains. He will trouble us no longer. The horse-clans will see to him all the rest of his days."

At his words, the clan chief gestured. Two of his warriors slipped from their mounts and took up the slumped figure of the shaman. A third rider led the shaman's horse to them. They lay his unresisting body over the horse's back, and secured him in place. The clan chief saluted Pendravyn and his company, then led his company of warriors away from the ruined city and back towards the mountain pass that would see them back to the horse clans and thence on to their homeland.

Sir Daven knelt on one knee before Mykael. Squire Persiflas took the mailed helm from the knight and stood at attention beside him, the helm under one arm and Monsterslayer sheathed in his other hand. His blue eyes solemn for once, Sir Daven addressed Mykael.

"When I was but a young lad, no older than you, Master Mykael, I was brought into the service of my king. For many years I served him faithfully, and one day he brought me before my fellows and blessed me with his sword. On that day, I became a knight.

"Let it be known henceforth, young Mykael, that we of this company salute your courage and your service to the king, the revered Aelfris. You truly have the courage of a knight for all your tender years!"

Squire Persiflas held out the mighty sword of power which he wielded with his constant companion. The knight drew out Monsterslayer and touched the great blade once to Mykael's right shoulder and once to his left, and then he raised the blade before him in a salute.

"From this day forth," Squire Persiflas intoned, "in this world you shall be known to all as the Knight of Aelfris! Your owl," he pointed to the delicate shape Mykael wore about his neck, "shall be the symbol of your wisdom and your courage!"

"Hurrah! Hurrah!" Nickolas and Joss cried together. Daniel kicked and gurgled in Joss' arms. Merys curtsied and Pendravyn saluted Mykael with a deep bow.

For once in his life, his cousin was speechless, but as always, he seemed to know just what to do. He put out his hand to Sir Daven, who rose and shook the small brown hand, then offered it to the squire.

"How could I do anything else," Mykael asked simply, "with my friends as an example?"

Sir Daven grinned.

"Come, m'boy," he clapped Mykael on the shoulder, "let us take our leave of Rex and Hesperius."

Pendravyn gestured to the others.

"And you, my fine young man," he rubbed Nickolas on the top of the head, "you shall henceforth be called 'Niccolo Piccolo'!"

Nickolas grinned and patted his pocket.

"You have ever stood ready to help me, Master Nickolas. Are you certain you are not a little wizard in disguise?"

"No-o!" Nickolas dodged under the wizard's arm and giggled.

"Well, then," Pendravyn told him, "just remember your piccolo's song will always sound sweetly in this world if ever you do play it. See!" He pointed at Nickolas' pocket which glowed with a bright, momentary light.

The little boy's eyes widened.

"It's like your magic, Master Pendravyn!" He bounced on his feet in his excitement.

"Of course," Pendravyn smiled an reached out to ruffle Nickolas' hair.

Merys put her arm around Joss' shoulders.

"You are the three best friends that any wizard or lady witch might have," she declared, "but this little babe," she tickled Daniel on the cheek as he leaned forward for a kiss, "needs must go home to his father and mother, yes?"

"Yes," Joss answered. "But what will happen to the sim . . . simu . . . ."

"Simulacrum," Merys finished for him. "It is not real, young Joss. When this babe is returned, it will simply disappear."

"Good-bye, Master Pendravyn," Joss called. "Thank you for letting us help you to rescue Daniel and stop Khasil." For a moment, his gaze followed the Cherdir horsemen as they rode away from the ruined city.

"Ah, my lad," Pendravyn followed Joss' gaze, then he gave a crooked grin, "could I do less for my three apprentices? Now, come close, and we shall see you home again to Caristoke."

Whether Pendravyn actually said 'until next time,' or whether Joss had finally read the wizard's mind, he was not sure. When he stepped back from the wizard's embrace with Nickolas and Mykael, he found himself in the garden with his brother and his cousins, Brigady jumping and yipping at their feet.

Aunt Jasmin came up the garden path.

"Are you boys still playing in the garden?" She stopped to give them all a hug. "And what are you doing with Daniel out here? Come here, baby," she cooed at Daniel and took the sleepy baby from his cousin. "Let's take you home safe and sound. Tell your mother that I was by, and don't stay out too long," Aunt Jasmin reminded her nephews.

"Safe and sound!" Nickolas echoed with a hoot of laughter when she had gone, and the three boys guffawed.

"Wait until Daniel can talk!" Mykael gasped, holding his side.

"Who would believe it?" Joss sputtered. "Let's go see if our mother needs anything from the market. Maybe she'll have a tabutz to spare for treats."

"Hurrah!"

For a moment, as his brother and cousin and Brigady raced ahead of him, Joss' fingers stroked the dragon pinned to his collar, and he repeated softly under his breath, "until next time."

Wolverness Abbey

The Mother Superior's measuring gaze met Sister Condetta's worried eyes over Cailie's still form and nodded once. Cailie's breathing was shallow and rasping. Her covering had been pulled back, water bottles removed to expose skin. The Mother Superior placed a hand against Cailie's bared skin. Her body felt cool to the touch although the water bottles were still hot and the room was stifling in the heat from the fireplace and the steaming kettle of water.

Sister Condetta's sharp gaze raked the young novices and sisters filling ever more water bottles as fast as they could.

"Leave us," she ordered. The novices and young sisters went at once in a flutter of black robes, pulling the door shut behind them.

The Mother Superior closed her eyes and clasped the cross on her chest with both hands.

"Will you come?" She sent the silent question winging like a prayer.

A stillness in the room warned her as she opened her eyes and searched.

"I am here." A cloaked figure stepped out of shadow and came forward, tall and grave.

"She is nearly spent, her spirit has begun its journey home to our Lord." The Mother Superior motioned to Cailie. "We can do no more for her."

The man knelt at once by Cailie's bedside and took her hands in his, and Sister Condetta, praying, watched and wondered. The moment he touched Cailie's hands, it seemed to her that the room in which they stood dissolved and they were in the midst of an ancient forest, whose trees were so old and so tall that light was filtered from a long way down, their boles thick, existing outside of time. A whisper of wind, barely felt, touched her face and hands, as if sorting out the who and what of her body and her soul. Sister Condetta closed her eyes and prayed harder.

Mother Superior prayed, too, but she kept her eyes open. There were many paths for the Lord's blessings and mercy to follow, and this man, she had decided long ago, when a cloaked shadow had first answered her most desperate prayer over a sick child's bedside, was one such way. He had called himself the Catcher of Sorrows, and when he came—other times—he brought with him the gift of peace even when he could not help her save a life. But never before had he brought them all into such a place as this! Always before, his strength and power had been centered in the sickroom.

His head bowed, he held Cailie's hands tightly and out of him flowed not despair, but an awareness of the universe and the place of all life within it. It rooted him here in this moment and this place and from it he gained both strength and patience. The ancient forest responded to him, sighed, held time slowed, and drew Cailie's soul from out of the darkness and the cold, guiding it home again to Wolverness Abbey and into her body.

When he lifted his head from her hands, his face was more drawn and white than the Mother Superior ever remembered seeing him, but he did not rise at once. They were back in the abbey sickroom, all of them. Beside her, she felt Sister Condetta start as Cailie's eyelids fluttered and put a warning hand on the sister's arm before she could speak.

Blue eyes stared for a moment into eyes as deep and dark as pools of night, but warmed by tenderness, then the Catcher of Sorrows was rising, the cloak floating about him like warm air, and he was gone. Cailie half-rose from her bed, one hand grasping for the edge of his cloak as it disappeared into thin air.

"No!" she cried brokenly. "Pendarek! No! No!" Then she buried her face in her pillow as hard, wrenching sobs wracked her body.

Mother Superior touched Sister Condetta's arm.

"Quickly, Sister Condetta. Bring a cup of the *sièlhan* from Sister Carmena."

Sister Condetta went swiftly from the sick room to fetch the *sièlhan*—a hot, honeyed drink, strong with herbs, to soothe mind and body. It would give this patient rest. The Mother Superior wondered at what she had just witnessed, but did not voice her thoughts aloud. Sitting on the edge of Cailie's bed, she held her patient gently and let Cailie cry. The Catcher of Sorrows had gone, but not before the Mother Superior glimpsed the pain it had cost him to leave. She prayed, as she stroked Cailie's head, that wherever he had gone, comfort would await him, for surely, two hearts lay broken at his leaving.